REDEEMING GRACE

Gina Salamon

REDEEMING GRACE

PUBLISHING HISTORY
First Edition: October 2019

ISBN-13:978-1699298459

Printed in the United States of America

This one's for my daughter,
whose love of anything Christmas,
books, movies, you name it,
inspire me every day.

Welcome to
St. Thaddaeus

If you're feeling lost, lonely, or simply searching, but for what you aren't quite sure, you might want to take a trip through the Rocky Mountains of Colorado.

There, nestled between peaks and valleys, not hidden, nor easily found, sits the Town of Saint Thaddaeus.

Now, you won't find Saint Thad—as we locals call it—on any map, old or new. Nor will that GPS of yours, or any internet search help you. And although I live in Saint Thad, and have for many a year, I can't be giving you exact directions.

I can, however, tell you that if you travel northwest of Denver and stay on the main roads, and, *if* you are meant to find us, you will.

Because the signs will all be there.

CHAPTER 1

The unexpected blare of an alarm notifying all within earshot of incoming traffic nearly had Mary Francis jumping clear out of her flat-soled shoes.

"Sweet heavens to Betsy," Mary Francis exclaimed while inspecting the new hairline fracture in the coffee pot she had banged against the faucet. Mumbling under her breath, she grabbed a kitchen towel and rushed back to her desk to punch in the necessary code that would bring the highway camera up on her monitor.

A silver hatchback filled the screen, its speed slow and steady as snow had begun to fall at an increasing rate. With another keystroke, the driver's face came into close up.

Female, this time around and young. "Well, it's about time." Finally, a lost soul she could sink her wingtips into.

As the town's new apprentice, Mary Francis had been assigned only a handful of souls so far, all of them male and most over forty. A mere coincidence or just happenstance, of course, but she couldn't help secretly wanting a little variety.

Taking a closer look at the monitor, she saw the woman on the screen looked to be barely past her mid-twenties and was gnawing on her bottom lip, her anxious green eyes darting over the roadway as both hands white-knuckled the steering wheel.

"Poor, sweet child." Mary Francis *tsk*ed and shook her head.

Not another moment passed before her supervisor appeared, his lanky torso leaning over her shoulder to view the image on the screen.

"Hmm," he murmured in apparent satisfaction.

"Now, was a snowstorm all that necessary?" she asked, looking up at him with a furrowed brow. "Cause I'm thinking this poor child looks mighty uncomfortable on that slippery road."

The supervisor's lips twisted into a frown. "It's not me who arranges to get 'em here, Mary Francis, but apparently so."

She acknowledged that statement with a roll of her eyes. "Well, seeing as it's comin' on Christmas, I'm supposin' I shouldn't be surprised, but since when were we expectin' a new arrival?"

"As of about an hour ago. I would have told you sooner if my meeting hadn't run so long."

Mary Francis stifled a chortle. "Judgin' by the powdered sugar on your upper lip, I'm guessin' Virginia May brought baked goods again?"

In response to the teasing remark, he dropped a handful of papers beside the apprentice's keyboard with a soft *thwack*, and at the same time, pulled a handkerchief from the pocket of his pants, promptly disposing of the evidence of his overindulgent sweet tooth.

"That's everything you need to know about our new arrival," he said, his tone flat and no-nonsense.

Fully aware that now was not the time to digest the background of their newest soul, Mary Francis merely scanned the pages. "Mercy me," she said, followed by a cluck of her tongue. "No wonder this child needs our help. You thinkin' we'll have more than the usual day or two with this one? 'Cause I'm thinkin' we sure as ever are gonna need it."

"From what you'll see in there," he said with a nod indicating the papers, "keeping her here long enough will be part of the challenge.

Although, I'm pretty confident more than a few days shouldn't be too difficult to manage. You up for it?"

"Oh, you betcha, I am! Why I've been achin' for just this thing."

"Well, post the signs then, and let's get started."

CHAPTER 2

"I'm sorry I wasn't here to take your call, but please leave a message—"

Grace clicked off and dropped the phone into her console, allowing a pent-up breath to seep from between her clenched teeth.

A glance at her surroundings nearly had her growling in frustration. "Only you would go haring off without a plan."

Then again, didn't she always?

According to her smartphone's GPS, the nearest gas station was another fifty miles ahead. Fifty miles, that according to said phone, would take one hour, fourteen minutes in this mountainous terrain.

Although blankets of white covered the rocky scenery, and the stone monuments in the near distance were snow-capped and frozen, the roads were clear and dry and had been since she left Denver. However, judging by the icy flakes striking her windshield at an increasingly rapid rate, that was about to change.

"You just *had* to choose the cusp of winter," Grace muttered to herself. But she'd stayed too long this last time; longer than any of the other places she'd set down since leaving Ohio and it was well past time.

Pittsburgh, Baltimore, Richmond. She'd sampled each. Next came Atlanta, then Jacksonville, where she discovered the deep south was no place for her. She most definitely was not one for year-round heat and humidity. From there, she moved on to Shreveport for a brief time, followed by Dallas, Pueblo, and, most recently, Denver.

She'd been debating on where to try next, considering either Wyoming, Utah, or Idaho, and planned to make a decision by the time she reached the northern border of Colorado. But first, she would have to get there.

Flicking another glance at her gas gage, Grace inwardly chastised herself and seriously considered turning around. For all the good that would do, the last gas station she passed was a good forty minutes behind her.

A sudden chill sent a shiver from her toes to her ears and warned the outside temperature was dropping, as did the fogging of her windows. She hit the defrost, leaned forward to swipe at the glass with her hand, and caught sight of a blue road sign.

Gas, food, and lodging, five miles ahead? How could that be?

Although Grace slowed to get a better look, nothing about the sign changed. She figured she either had to be seeing what was nothing more than a mirage brought on by anxiety—the cause of which was pure stupidity on her part—or some juvenile delinquents had managed to camouflage a zero. Then she saw the small billboard just beyond that first sign.

PAT'S HOAGIES
Best Meatball Sandwich West of Philly!
Center of Town Square - Just Five Miles Ahead

She gave the smartphone in her console a disgruntled frown.

Following the billboard's instructions, Grace pulled off at the next exit where, at first glance, she saw not an iota's evidence of civilization, not one man-made structure, or even a cleared field for farming or ranching. And now that she thought about it, neither did she see a single soul or another automobile other than her own.

The lack had a ball of apprehension forming in her belly, but taking her depleted fuel into consideration, Grace ignored the uneasy feeling and continued on.

The new route took her down a winding two-lane road shrouded by thick groves of evergreens on either side. A welcome relief after so many miles of frozen rock, even with the disquieting sense that something wasn't quite as it seemed.

A mile or two further, and finally, the trees began to thin. Then an old-fashioned street lamp backed by a pair of conical evergreens came into view.

With twilight having arrived by this time, the steadily falling snow shimmered like crystals and gave the entire scene created by the carved wooden marker below an ethereal glow. It read:

Welcome to
St. Thaddaeus
A Town of Redeeming Grace

Her heart stuttered.

Beyond that sign lay a wide valley, the sight no less Americana than a Hargrove painting. Acres and acres of trees spread wide over the hills to the east, and below them lay a dotting of houses.

In the foreground, Grace stared in awe at what had to be town square, where one quaint storefront after another lined a paved roadway.

Glancing left and right at the sight just ahead, she saw that nearly every store window looked to be filled with twinkling lights and gaudy holiday decorations. Some were dressed in the usual colors of fall as Thanksgiving was only days away, while a few others sported the traditional blue and silver Hanukkah fair, and the rest were already dressed for Christmas.

In the middle of the square, a massive blue spruce set the stage fronted by a raised circle that held a large fountain. Perched atop that fountain, a stone statue stood tall and proud, a pair of angel wings protruding from its back.

Grace blinked, wholly expecting the entire scene would disappear before her eyes, but nothing did.

"I've stumbled onto the set of a cheesy *Hallmark* movie."

From a four-way stop, she glanced this way and that, searching for some indication of which way would lead her to a gas station. Her gaze fell on a man and two small children passing the angel statue, the three of them appearing to be watching a pair of squirrels chase each other around the trunk of a fat denuded tree.

The children wore bright winter coats with matching knit caps and thick woolen mittens, whereas the gentleman was covered in varying shades of brown ranging from caramel to dark chocolate. With both surprise and delight, Grace noted each wore a scarf that half-covered their face; scarves made to look like caricature masks.

Dismissing the tug on her heart, she pulled to the curb and rolled down her passenger-side window. "Excuse me!" she called out. "Could you point me in the direction of the nearest gas station?"

As the adult looked up in her direction, Grace saw more clearly that the mask he wore depicted a goatee-wearing character with bad teeth and a cigar in his mouth.

Comical and off-putting at the same time, if you ask me.

The man instantly stepped to the curb and leaned in her open passenger window with the palm of one hand resting on the roof.

Grace couldn't quite make out the color of the man's eyes, the only part of his face that was visible, in the diffused light, but didn't miss the way he looked her over before speaking.

"Only one gas station in St Thad. You'll want to keep going straight through the square, past Aspen there," he added with a jerk of his thumb. "Station's on your left, next block over."

He didn't bother to lower the scarf as he spoke, which was just as well, Grace thought, although a little disconcerting.

Pushing a honey-blonde curl behind her ear, she murmured her thanks and was just about to roll up her window and pull back into the street when he said, "You won't be able to get any gas tonight if that's what you're after. Mac closed down, not five minutes ago. Says this storm is coming in fast. If I were you, I'd be heading home." He paused. "Then again, I don't guess you're from around here, are you?"

Grace didn't bother to reply to what she took as a rhetorical question. Instead, she nibbled on her bottom lip and considered her choices.

Driving on a deserted highway at night wasn't on her list of enjoyable pastimes, especially in weather such as this. Plus, she hadn't eaten all day and had hoped to pick something up before starting out again. But if this "Mac" knows what he's talking about, and by the looks of things, he just might, even a minute's delay, would be unwise.

Grace's gaze reconnected with the good Samaritan. "The sign on the highway said you've got lodging in town?"

He tilted his head. "Mac's aunt runs a nice bed and breakfast. Just maneuver on around the square until you're back on Sycamore, that's the crossroad behind you, then hang a right. Top of the hill, you'll see a blue Victorian. Hard to miss."

Grace nodded and put her car in gear. "Oh, the meatball hoagies. Are they as good as the billboard boasts?"

Amusement shown in the man's eyes as he squinted at her through the flakes now covering his lashes and brows. Whether it was her the good Samaritan found amusing, or the happy squeals of the children behind him, Grace could only guess.

"Billboard must be new," he said, "but if you're talking about Pat's, his meatballs are a definite favorite." The man turned to glance over his shoulder. "Still open by the looks of it. Pat's is just behind me."

"Thanks. I appreciate your help."

"Any time." And with a mock tip of his hat, the man turned back to his children.

Shrugging off a sudden sense of...well, of something she couldn't quite identify, Grace pulled into the street. Nearly mesmerized by the holiday displays in the shop windows, she moved at a crawl while taking note of all the small town had to offer.

Lily's Unique Boutique, Carmine's Barber Shop, and Dewley's Diner appeared to be closed up tight, others following suit as Grace saw a few lights go out.

She turned onto Linden, pulled into an empty parking slot two doors down from Pat's Hoagies, and bracing for the expected blast of frigid air, she tucked her knitted scarf securely around her neck and climbed out from behind the wheel.

At that same moment, a shopper spilled out onto the sidewalk, her hands filled with packages. Her round frame teetered when a sudden gust of wind kicked up, sending one of her purchases to the ground.

"Sweet heavens to Betsy!"

"I've got it." Grace rushed to the woman's side to retrieve the dropped book from the ground, taking note of the title before handing it back. "The DoGoodie Series. Excellent choice."

"You think?" the frazzled woman asked with pursed lips. "Took me near on half an hour to make up my mind, and I'm still not convinced."

"The series is very popular among children ages six to ten."

The shopper's entire face lit up. Her dark-chocolate eyes gleamed with a sense of whimsy, and her smooth umber skin radiated with warmth. That harassed exterior now gone, she seemed perfectly willing to stand on an icy sidewalk with snow steadily coming down on her head and shoulders until she was knee-deep in it.

"You sound like someone who's got experience with these things," the woman said. "But, honey, you look way too young to have a child that age. Your kin, maybe?"

"Uh, no," Grace replied. "I've spent the last several years working in bookstores, though."

"Well, '*thank the Lord*' is what Charlie's gonna be shouting soon as you git yourself on inside."

"Excuse me?"

The woman nodded toward the window behind her, sending Grace's gaze over the gold block letters spread across the glass that read BARKER'S BOOKS, and in the bottom left hand corner, a small HELP WANTED sign.

A familiar voice echoed through Grace's head. "*Watch for the signs, and God will lead you home.*"

Now, in the whole of her twenty-six years, Grace had never quite decided whether or not she truly believed in the Almighty, and she might be a bit dense now and again, not that she'd ever admit that out loud, but she was by no means blind.

Someone was trying to tell her something.

And although she had long ago resigned herself to never finding a place she could truly call home, the voice in her head was one Grace never could ignore.

"You had best hurry on in there, Honey," the woman said, breaking into Grace's thoughts. "Charlie done told me he was gittin' ready to close up for the night. And *goodness*, but he'll be sleepin' like a babe with a full belly once he knows he's got the help he's been a prayin' for before the holiday rush gits full of steam."

Grace gave the sign in the window another glance and once again considered her options.

11

CHAPTER 3

The sound of muffled laughter and a mingle of voices rose up through the heating vents in the floor. A curious thing, those voices, Grace mused from her seat before the writing desk in her rented room. When she'd arrived inquiring about staying for the night, Virginia, the proprietor of the B&B, told Grace she was their only guest, and here it was barely half-past six in the morning the following day!

Perhaps, the sudden storm had brought in a few more unsuspecting travelers?

She listened for a long moment, attempting to distinguish a word or two, before turning back to her letter writing with a shrug.

...So how did I end up here, you might ask. Well, my plan was to gas up, eat, and get back on the road. That was, until what started out as gently falling snow morphed into blinding white blurs. Then there were the signs and your voice in my head, and well, here I am, even if I'm still not quite sure why.

I know, why did I leave Denver in the first place? Just refer to my most recent letters, and you'll know it's because, with each passing day, I was getting closer to the edge. I recognize the signs well enough, and if I'd stayed, it would have started happening again. You know as well as I do I'm right about that. So, here I am, disappointing you once again.

Anyway, this stop will be even more temporary than usual—just through the holidays, so it really doesn't count. The town is called St. Thaddaeus, and it's far from what I'm used to. I spent the night in a B&B, the only available lodging as it turns out. It's a grand Victorian with a huge front porch, wide moldings, and scalloped trim. The inside looks just as you'd imagine, too, with period-style furnishings. As a matter-of-fact, the writing desk I'm sitting at is nearly identical to the one Mr. Matthews donated to the rectory.

So, the plan now is to count on anonymity to get me through. The few people I've met so far have been more than welcoming, which, of course, makes staying even for a short while both simple and difficult at the same time.

Then again, I'm sure you'd say I've gotten a bit too good at keeping things simple, even if I can't manage it for long.

13

Missing you,

Grace

She slipped the letter into an envelope before tucking it into a pocket of her jeans and headed downstairs.

There she found her hostess in the breakfast room, chatting with a woman slumped at one of four small tables. Behind them, two men, both over fifty, if they were a day, occupied another.

The man on the left sat comfortably slouched, a pale Stetson in his lap and gesturing wildly with a fork, while his grim-faced companion sipped from a mug shaped like the head of a deer.

Grace returned her gaze to the younger woman who looked to have just come off a twelve-hour night shift. Her dark eyes were bloodshot, her lids heavy, and her posture so relaxed that Grace thought it a monumental feat the woman hadn't slid to the floor.

She was dressed in a heavy sweater, grease-stained jacket, snow boots, and soft-worn jeans. The knitted cap at her elbow explained the disheveled dark auburn hair that gave the impression she'd just climbed out of bed.

The young woman flicked her chin in Grace's direction, which in turn had the B&B owner following the woman's gaze.

"Well, good morning!" Virginia called out as she motioned for Grace to join them. "You're certainly up and about earlier than I expected you'd be. Sit down here with my niece, and I'll get you a plate."

"Oh, no, I just—" Grace got out no more than that before Virginia disappeared through a swinging door.

"Mackenzie," the young woman said by way of a greeting, "but you can call me Mac, everyone else does. And you might as well sit down because no matter what you might say otherwise, Aunt Ginnie's going to feed you."

14

Grace hesitated to accept the friendly invitation, but as she abhorred rudeness in others, she slipped a loose curl behind her ear, mumbled her own introduction, and pulled out a chair.

"Are you a guest here?" Grace asked. "At the B&B, I mean."

"Lived here, once upon a time," Mackenzie replied after taking a long gulp from her moose head mug. "I've got a place of my own now, but whenever work calls me out at some ungodly hour, I detour to Aunt Ginnie's for breakfast."

"Oh. What do you do that gets you up so early?"

"Depends on the day." Mac grinned. "For instance, I just spent the last four hours plowing the streets. After I've fortified myself with enough caffeine to get me through the next several hours, I'll open the station, and once my part-time help shows up, I can get to work replacing the radiator in Mr. Tucker's ancient Chevy pick-up."

"So, you're that Mac? The one who owns the gas station?"

The exhausted young woman nodded and covered a huge yawn with the palm of one hand. "I'm also the town mechanic and own the only tow truck within forty-some miles." Lifting her mug, Mac added, "Here's hoping you won't need that service while you're here."

"Hopefully not," Grace replied with a smile of her own. "I take it that puts you on call 24/7?"

"Mostly. My part-time help is a senior in high school, so I get a little relief now and then. Plus, there's always a willing fill-in around if I need some time off."

Across the room, one of the men cleared his throat, prompting Mac to wave a limp hand in their direction. "You're probably thinking we're all here to check you out," Mac said under her breath, "which, if I'm being honest, has a little truth to it on my part. Otherwise, I'd already have taken off. Those two show up here more often than I do, though, and pretty regularly. It's hard to resist Aunt Ginnie's pastries."

Grace chanced a glance at the gentlemen, and seeing the crumbs left on their plates decided Mac wasn't exaggerating.

The one with the deer head coffee mug caught her eye and crossed his arms over his narrow chest, his deep scowl at odds with his probing gaze, while the more pleasant-looking man rose and came forward to shake Grace's hand.

This one was tall, wide-shouldered, and pleasantly handsome for an older man, his thick gray hair creased by his Stetson. As he bent over her, Grace saw that his faded blue eyes were as warm as his smile.

"Duncan Haney. Welcome to St. Thad."

"Thank you," Grace murmured, her gaze flicking to the curmudgeon, whose subsequent greeting amounted to nothing more than a grunt.

"Don't mind Zee," Duncan said, flicking his chin in the direction of his companion as he resumed his seat. "He hasn't had his second cup of coffee yet."

To Grace's relief, Virginia came bustling back in then, a plate of assorted muffins in one hand, an empty coffee mug—this one a raccoon head—and a fresh pot of coffee in the other.

"How do you prefer your eggs, Grace? I can have some ready for you quick as butter melts."

Grace eyed the plate of sugary goodness. "I'm not really a morning person. A muffin will be plenty, and hot tea with milk if you have it?"

Virginia shook her head and clucked her tongue. "The tea's no problem, but breakfast is the most important—"

Mac snorted, effectively cutting her aunt off mid-sentence. "Let her be, Aunt Ginnie. You know as well as the rest of us, Grace'll never be able to stop at just one. She won't leave hungry."

The self-satisfied grin brought on by the boast of her baking skills transformed the B&B owner's well-worn features to those of someone years younger. "Well, that's true enough, but some protein to go with it only makes the day ahead a better one. That's what I always say." Virginia shifted her girth to reveal a double pair of watchful eyes. Atop her head, her ash-brown bun mixed with threads of gray wobbled.

"In case she hasn't already introduced herself," Virginia said to the room at large, "this here is Grace St. John, who, unlike our usual visitors, plans to take up residence in St. Thad. Don't you, Honey?"

"Um...just through the holidays." Not one to be shy, not typically; Grace was surprised to hear her own meek words. When she realized she was fidgeting, she mentally clamped herself down in the chair.

"Is that yours there, Grace?"

Following Virginia's gaze, Grace looked down to see her letter on the floor by her feet and quickly snatched it up. "Yes. Yes, it's a letter. I wrote it this morning. It must have fallen out of my pocket."

"Oh, well, give it here, and I'll see it goes out with the mail."

Grace tucked the envelope safely back in her pocket. "Actually, I don't report to the bookstore until two today, so I thought I'd take a tour of the town before then. You know, so I can familiarize myself with where everything is? I thought I'd make the post office one of my stops."

Taking a breath, she added, "I also planned to look for a place to rent. Week to week, if possible, or by the month at most. Furnished, of course. Is there a real estate agent in town or—"

"Why, you're welcome to stay here as long as you like, Grace."

"Oh, your place is beautiful, Virginia, and comfortable for sure, but I'm not much of a people person, really, and I sort of value my privacy," she finished, her voice losing strength with each word.

Virginia waved Grace's comment off as unimportant, while the man they called Zee decided to join the conversation. "First, you're not a morning person," he grumbled, "now you're not a people person. What kind of person are you, then?"

Grace could only stare with her mouth agape. She wasn't used to people prying, especially when they barely even knew her. And no one ever called her out on being aloof. Who wasn't these days?

"Well?" he asked with what amounted to a sneer.

Numerous witty replies buzzed around in Grace's brain, but not one made it as far as her mouth.

"Bah!" Zee swiped a hand through the air as if batting away a pesky bug. "A small town's no place for her," he said to the others. "What she wants is the big city where no one even knows her name."

"Sounds like a song I heard once," Virginia muttered.

Mac rolled her eyes. "More people, instead of less, Zee? How's that make sense for someone who just wants to be left alone?"

"You ever hear the saying 'lost in a crowd?'" he argued.

"There's the old Cambroto place out on Maple," Duncan put in.

Mac and Virginia exchanged a look Grace couldn't quite read. "You sure about that?" Virginia asked him.

Duncan took a drawn-out sip of coffee, leaving an awkward silence hanging in the air. "It's been empty long enough. No sense in it staying that way, and it certainly isn't fair to Florence who's got the burden of keeping that house standing."

He met Grace's gaze. "It's a small place, I'll grant you. Only two bedrooms, one bath, and it's on the far edge of town. But if it's privacy you're after, you'll get it."

"Sounds perfect," Grace responded. Then, noting the expressions on the other's faces, she couldn't help but ask, "You're *sure* it's available?"

"Positive," he said with a definitive nod. I'll give Florence a call here in just a bit, and you can go on over and have a look-see after you finish your breakfast."

Grace thanked Duncan for his help, and as the others moved on to more local topics of conversation, she took her first bite of a blueberry muffin that was possibly the best she'd ever tasted.

She'd found some comradery this morning, Grace mused with a surreptitious glance around the room. It was a good feeling, although one she knew better than to get comfortable with because the minute she did, things would change. Keeping her distance was always the best course of action, no matter how hard. And knowing she wouldn't be here long in any case, Grace had every intention of remembering that.

Yet she couldn't help but wonder at the odd pulse of...something not quite right in the room. An uncertainty or concern she noted in the other's eyes. She wanted to ask about it—she was sure Mac would explain—but adhering to the self-proclaimed vow to keep to herself, Grace decided it was best not to pry.

Pushing those thoughts to the back of her mind, she sunk her teeth into the still warm-from-the-oven sweetness, before following it with a sip from the cup of hot tea Virginia had placed in front of her. Mac topped off her mug of coffee, swearing it was her last for the day, then twisted in her chair in response to her aunt's mumbled question, something about an upcoming town event, while Duncan and Zee continued to converse in hushed tones; although from the scowls on both of their faces, she guessed it was more like a disagreement.

As Zee's grumbling tone reached a new level, Grace's gaze slid his way. Their eyes met, and with a jerk of his chin in her direction, Zee leaned toward Duncan and spoke from the side of his mouth.

Grace pulled her shoulders in and ducked her head. She couldn't quite make out the man's words, but judging by his unchanged expression, she didn't imagine he'd said anything complimentary.

CHAPTER 4

"If I didn't know better, I'd say you were a scrooge."

From her perch high on a ladder above her co-worker's head, Grace looked down at Allie Baldwin's lifted face with a snort of laughter. "I probably am what everyone in this town would consider a scrooge, and anyway, how well could you possibly know someone you met less than twenty-four hours ago?" It was only her second day on the job, and already Grace had found a friend she knew it would be difficult to say goodbye to when the time came. At least, that was the impression Allie gave her now, Grace reminded herself with an internal scolding.

"But I won't say that," Allie went on as if Grace hadn't spoken, "because I saw you with those rowdy Pulaski boys this morning, and anyone who can deal with Jesse Pulaski without wanting to spank his little behind has to be a saint. And saints don't boo-hoo Christmas."

Grace pretended to snuffle a laugh. "You might want to give that logic another go around in your head. What on earth do the Pulaski boys and Christmas possibly have to do with me turning down an invitation to Thanksgiving dinner?"

Allie's cupid's bow mouth twisted in thought. "Okay, so you got me there. Thanksgiving isn't a religious holiday, after all, it's an American one. You *were* born and raised in the United States, weren't you? I'm just asking because if not, I can understand you not being familiar with Thanksgiving—"

"Where I was born is up for debate and has nothing to do with it."

"What do you mean, "up for debate?""

"Never mind," Grace said, waving the question away as she checked the label on another carton of books.

The two were in the storeroom of the bookstore, searching for a special order that had been put aside for a customer. According to Allie, Lizbeth Haney—Duncan Haney's wife, as it turned out—purchased the Christmas gift some months ago. Allie was certain the store's owner had stashed the carton containing the special order on one of the uppermost shelves, and Charlie swore he'd labeled the box with the name "Haney" on the top flap. Still not finding what they were looking for, Grace climbed another two rungs.

"So, sure, not everyone celebrates Christmas," Allie went on, "I'll give you that. But how can you dislike Thanksgiving?"

Grace pushed aside another carton and sent a flurry of dust down to tickle her nose. From the corner of her eye, she saw a grouping of cobwebs within arm's reach and instantly recoiled.

"Careful," Allie warned while steadying the ladder. "I mean, Thanksgiving's nothing like Christmas. For my family, and if I'm not mistaken, this is pretty much universal, Turkey Day's a time to get together with friends and family, stuff our faces, watch football and just hang out. What's not to like about that?"

"Ah-ha! Here's the sucker." Grace handed the found treasure to Allie before starting down the ladder. Once at the bottom, she had to wait for Allie to move aside before she could dismount. Between Charlie's behemoth-sized desk and the metal shelving lining the walls, the windowless storeroom barely offered enough floor space for two people to occupy it at the same time. And going by the thin slash of Allie's mouth, she had no intention of moving until Grace gave her a satisfactory explanation for not budging in her conviction to spend Thanksgiving alone.

"Look," Grace said in a more serious tone. "The simple fact is, I just don't have any interest in stuffing my face. I also dislike football and have no family or friends that I care to hang out with, so..."

"Thanks a lot!" Allie accompanied her exclamation with a good-natured laugh, then stepped aside and set the box down on the desk at her back. "So, what you're telling me is, you won't join us tomorrow no matter how much I beg?"

"Ding, ding, ding. Give the girl fifty points." Grace began brushing the dust from her face and clothes before pulling the elastic band from her ponytail to shake out her curls, while Allie took a box cutter from a drawer and sliced open the top of the carton.

"What is this special order, anyway?" Grace asked, conveniently changing the subject.

"The complete works of Arthur Conan Doyle."

Grace let out an inelegant snort. "Well, *that's* not what I expected."

"You were thinking something more along the lines of Louis L'Amour or Zane Grey, right?"

"How'd you guess?"

"Never judge a man by his hat, Grace."

"Speaking of which, does Mr. Haney always wear that over-sized cowboy hat?"

"Winter, spring, summer, and fall. I hear he was born and bred on a ranch in Wyoming, and I guess the uniform stuck. But look what else we've got in here." Allie pulled a second stack of hardbound books from beneath the thick leather-bound volumes. "About the same time Mrs. Haney placed this order for her husband, Mr. Haney came in and asked Charlie to order these for his wife. It seems both had the same idea this year as far as Christmas presents."

Grace inspected the cover of one of the books from the second stack. "Romance novels? Seriously?"

Allie shrugged. "Lizbeth Haney has a thing for men in kilts, which you'll learn soon enough hanging around here.

"Now me," she continued, "I prefer the very arrogant and extremely possessive English lords of the eighteenth and nineteenth centuries. Put me in a bubble bath with a regency romance and a glass of wine, and I'm in heaven. How about you, Grace? Favorite genre and perfect man?"

"I only read true crime," Grace lied. "As for the perfect man... No such animal. Not for me."

"Oh, you're just—" Allie began with laughter in her voice, but after a single glance at Grace's serious face, she shut her mouth and started again. "Oh, you mean like that."

Now it was Grace's turn to laugh. "No, I don't mean like that. Anyway," Grace rushed on before Allie could question her further, "I can understand the attraction for someone in Mrs. Haney's shoes, so I won't hold the indulgence against her."

"What shoes?" Allie asked, wrinkling her brow.

Grace let out an unladylike snort. "I've run into Duncan Haney no less than four times in the past two days (which is pretty weird in itself if you ask me), and every one of those times he's had that grump they call Zee with him. If Mrs. Haney has to put up with that old goat on a daily basis, it's no wonder she needs a little fantasy in her life."

Allie choked on a laugh, her dark brown eyes glistening with humor as she began handing the books off to Grace one at a time, her short, dark bob swaying with every move. Grace thought the cut went perfectly with Allie's pixie-like features and petite frame.

"I have to say, Grace, it surprises me you'd say that. Zee's always been friendly from what I've seen. Maybe he just needs a few days to warm up to you."

"Warm up? Allie, the man does nothing but sneer every time he sees me, and I've barely said a word to him."

"Maybe that's the problem." Once the box was empty, Allie turned to gather a large stack of holiday shopping bags Charlie had asked for.

"Whatever." Glad she'd managed to divert her co-worker's attention from not just one taboo subject, but two—those being the holidays and members of the opposite sex—Grace waved away all thoughts of the unpleasant man and pushed open the storeroom door.

As Allie followed Grace with her share of the Haneys' purchases and a few dozen shopping bags tucked under her arm, she said, "You know, Grace, I think you're imagining those sneers. Honestly, Zee's the sweetest man."

After reaching the front counter, Grace relieved herself of her burden, then quickly snatched up a Barker's Books' shopping bag from under the counter.

During her impromptu job interview, Grace learned that the store logo emblazoned on the bag, which sported a large, hairy dog holding a book in his mouth, wasn't simply a figment of the imagination of some advertising company, but a real, live mascot who occasionally made personal appearances as a treat for the local children.

"Oh, don't use that one," Allie scolded, "use this." Stuffing all but one of her finds from the storeroom under the counter, Allie held the remaining holiday bag up to show off the artwork that adorned both the front and back. It was a watercolor drawing of Santa Claus handing out books to a group of adoring children with the Barker's Books' mascot standing tall and proud, tongue lolling, at the cheery elf's side.

"I did tell you Mrs. Haney's the school librarian, didn't I?" Allie asked. "Or, town librarian, I guess you'd say, as we only have the one."

"One library or one school?" Grace hid her amusement by ducking her head as she carefully tied a gift tag to the shopping bag containing Duncan Haney's order. Allie changed subjects faster than a hot knife cut through butter.

"Both. St. Thaddaeus School houses pre-school through grade twelve, and our only library is connected to it. I mean, physically, connected. See, the library's nowhere near as old as the school is, and technically they're next door to each other; but then the town added this covered walkway a few years back that connects the two buildings so the kids can get from one to the other without having to worry about the weather."

Grace unfolded a second holiday sack and began filling it with the Arthur Conan Doyle volumes. The bell over the front door jangled.

"Quick, Grace, hide the Scottish hunks!" Allie said under her breath before calling out with a friendly wave, "Hey, Mrs. Haney. Hi kids. Go on back and make yourselves comfortable. Storytime's coming right up."

"That's the Haney twins," Allie explained as Lizbeth Haney led a small boy and girl toward the rear of the store. "Such a sad story there," she whispered.

"Oh, and in case Charlie forgot to tell you, any day there's no school, holidays excluded, of course, Barker's Books hosts storytime. One o'clock on the dot."

Grace tore her gaze from the twins as they disappeared among the shelves. "Uh, yeah, he filled me in. Charlie also asked if I'd do the honors if he didn't get back from the dentist in time. You don't mind, do you?"

"Are you kidding?" Allie asked with a dramatic roll of her eyes. "Not with the Pulaski boys in house. You know, I don't think your old boss realized Barker's Books is as small as it is when he told Charlie he should make you head of the children's department. As good as you are with kids, it's a shame you don't have any of your own."

A twinge of longing struck Grace at the reminder of the job she'd left behind, not to mention the people she'd gotten to know a little too well, particularly the few children who made a habit of seeking her out whenever they visited the store.

"Does that mean I'll get to meet your little boy today?"

Allie shook her head. "I seriously doubt it. Jonathan's mother takes care of Connor while I work. Which is great, don't get me wrong, but nothing short of a dire emergency will get that woman out on the roads when there's snow on the ground."

Lowering her voice, Allie said, "Getting back to Mr. and Mrs. Haney's love life—"

"Since when were we talking about anyone's love life?"

"That's where I was going before Lizbeth Haney walked in. You see, Mr. Haney owns the hardware store—that's Haney's Hardware and Appliances around the corner on Blue Spruce—and for as far back as I can remember he would close the store every day at noon so he could meet Mrs. Haney in the park for lunch."

"But now he has lunch with his good buddy, Zee?"

"No, Smarty Pants. The Haneys still have lunch in the park, like always, but now that their younger son is back and pretty much running the place, Duncan doesn't have to close up in the middle of the day. *And*," Allie added with emphasis, "they take a stroll through the park in the evenings after dinner. Weather permitting, of course. Matter-of-fact, I ran into them there just last week. The snow hadn't come yet, and the Haneys were holding hands and laughing. It was the sweetest thing I've ever seen."

"All show," Grace muttered, unable to keep the thought to herself. When Allie gave her a questioning look, Grace shrugged. "I've seen it plenty of times before. Outside, people present the picture of bliss, but what goes on behind closed doors would make you shutter."

Allie shoved a hand on her hip. "You know, I'm beginning to see your problem, Grace St. John. You haven't found your happily-ever-after."

Grace scoffed. "Like I said, I don't do fiction. There's no such thing as happily-ever-after, or even happy-for-now if you ask me, and anyone who thinks otherwise is kidding themselves."

A customer appeared at the cash register then, just as three more came in the door with kids in tow. Grace placed the bag holding Mrs. Haney's special order on a shelf under the counter.

"Looks like I better get to picking out a book for storytime. You'll be all right here until Charlie gets back?"

"Sure." Allie looked like she wanted to say more when the sounds of tumbling merchandise drew everyone's attention.

Grace rushed into the fray, fully expecting to find one or more of the Pulaski boys at the center. What she found, instead, was Lizbeth Haney, a petite, handsome woman with short platinum-blonde hair fluttering around dozens of boxed Christmas cards now scattered across the center aisle, waving her arms in the air. Of course, the three Pulaski boys, with their matching sandy-colored hair and faces full of freckles, stood by guffawing and slapping their thighs with glee.

"What in the world have you two done?" Bent over the twins' bowed heads, Mrs. Haney continued to scold. The matching solemn expressions on the twins' faces indicated remorse for whatever part they'd played in the mishap, and Grace knew immediately what she needed to do.

Keeping to the sidelines for a moment longer while she assessed the situation—figuring the twins were safe as long as Mrs. Haney remained inside the store—Grace came up behind the oldest of the Pulaski boys and placed a hand on his shoulder.

"Jesse, why don't you go on back and choose a book for me?"

His amusement disappeared almost immediately with her touch, but the tears of laughter in his eyes remained as Jesse Pulaski stared up at Grace. "But I want to see—"

"There's nothing to see. So unless you want to help clean up...?"

"No way! I didn't do nothing."

"All right, then. Go on back and pick out a story you think everyone will enjoy. In fact, why don't you and your brothers each choose a book and then I'll pick from there? I'll only be a minute."

"Oh, all right." With one last snuffle of laughter and a well-aimed haughty smirk toward the twins, Jesse did as Grace asked, taking his younger brothers with him.

Turning her attention to Mrs. Haney, Grace broke into the woman's finger-shaking lecture by holding out her hand in greeting. "Hi. I'm Grace, Charlie's holiday help. Mrs. Haney, if you wouldn't mind, could you check on the Pulaski boys for me? I've instructed them each to choose a book for storytime, and from what I hear, you're the most qualified person to see they choose wisely."

"Oh, but I really should—"

"No, no, I've got this." Grace nodded toward the mess. "Besides, you're much better equipped for choosing literature than I am."

"Call me, Lizbeth, please," the older woman said, offering a tentative smile. "And only if you're sure? I'm so sorry about this. I swear I'd turned my back for less than a minute."

"I'm sure that's true. And don't worry, the twins and I will take care of it. You go on back."

"Well, all right, then." Narrowing her eyes, Lizbeth gave the twins one last quick scolding before removing herself from the scene.

Grace got down on her haunches to give the little ones her full attention and stretched her smile as wide as it would go. "I think I can guess what you both had in mind here, and it looks like a rather excellent idea to me. How about I give you a hand?"

CHAPTER 5

"I should have guessed." With one last scowl at the darkened store window, Grace shoved her frozen fingers in the pockets of her winter coat and stomped down the empty sidewalk.

It was either that or throw something. Although why she'd thought it even remotely possible the hardware store—or any store in this town for that matter—would be open on Thanksgiving Day, she didn't know.

Taking Duncan Haney up on his recommendation, Grace had followed him to meet with Florence, her new landlord, after breakfast that first morning. The woman appeared unsure at first, looking to Duncan for approval before agreeing on a week to week lease, and Duncan's apparent relief over the short-term arrangement, heightening Grace's curiosity all the more.

She was tempted to ask Duncan about his relationship with Florence and why his opinion mattered one way or the other but didn't. After all, she certainly didn't like people asking questions about *her* personal business, so why pry into theirs.

By noon that same day, she had checked out of the B&B and settled into the old house on the far edge of town. Now she could kick herself for being so hasty and for more reasons than she cared to think about.

The house was old, and a bit neglected but nowhere near falling down. It was quite charming, really, and although small, it was plenty large enough for one or two people. *As long as those two are a couple, that is.* That was a disclaimer Grace felt needed to be made, even if only in her own mind because the presence in the house with her since the night she'd moved in sometimes had her feeling quite crowded.

All that aside, and she chose not to think about it just now, the real problem wasn't so much the house itself, but its location.

With a population of just over five thousand, St. Thaddaeus wasn't big enough to boast big box stores, leaving Haney's Hardware and Appliances the only alternative for finding what she needed to unclog a drain. Even the local grocery store didn't carry the stuff! And wasn't it just her luck that the kitchen sink chose last night to back up?

Grace considered contacting her landlord, who might happen to have some of that liquid stuff on hand until she remembered Florence had gone out of town to meet relatives in Black Hawk for a few days of gambling. Grace also considered knocking on the door of a neighbor but didn't want to disrupt anyone's holiday celebrations. Plus, you never knew what you might be walking into. So, unless she wanted to get in her car and travel an hour or more one way to the nearest town that *did* boast one of those big chain stores, tonight she'd be washing dishes in the bathroom.

"Probably hiding in there all evening, too," she muttered under her breath, "just to avoid the noxious smell."

The weather had been mild throughout the day with temperatures hovering somewhere in the high forties and barely a breeze. Feeling unsettled, Grace had chosen to walk into town by way of its main park.

Just a few blocks east of the town's core, Araqiel Park took up forty-two acres of land, according to Allie, who also informed Grace it was Kutiel River that ran through the park's center.

With all the years she'd spent in parochial school and the many long conversations with Father, Grace knew an angel name when she heard one. And she was quickly learning that the people of St. Thad—or the town's founders, at any rate—had a thing for them.

According to Allie's boasts, Araqiel Park featured a series of paved paths that wound through an array of flower gardens (currently buried in snow and in hibernation) with benches interspersed along the way. It also housed a playground, two basketball courts, a ballpark, and skate park, all surrounded by vast green lawns. Of course, the latter was currently in the same state as its flower gardens.

Deserted as the town was on this holiday, and with nothing but her thoughts to accompany her, the crunch of snow beneath Grace's feet gave her a feeling of not being quite so alone even though there wasn't another soul in sight. And as she neared the park from this side of town, its charm embraced her with welcoming arms.

Her, a woman who harbored no fantasies that life indeed offered any such charms. None that lasted beyond the immediate present, anyway, or went deeper than a person's outer shell.

Of course, there were exceptions, but people that true were few and hard to find among all the fakers and takers, as she called them. A lesson Grace had learned early and taught herself not to forget.

But there lay memories she couldn't allow to linger, not when she was alone and susceptible. With a determined shake of her head Grace tried pulling her thoughts back to the present, but with the next slap of her boot on the snow-packed ground came a *crunch* that had her jumping back a step.

Kneeling, she found the tip of a broken bottle, its end jagged and raw. As she gathered the piece in the palm of her hand, tears of pent up frustration and loneliness began to stream down her face. Intent on begging for strength, she closed her eyes. But instead of resolve and stability, it was the memories she tried to forget that came flooding in, filling every recess of her mind.

She didn't pull the cell phone from her pocket this time, but just needing to hear his voice, even if only in her head, she imagined pulling up the number and listening to it ring.

"I'm sorry I wasn't here to take your call, but please leave a message, and I promise to get back to you as soon as I can."

31

How long she sat in that position, Grace wasn't sure, and whether it was the damp chill that had soaked through the knees of her jeans or the whimper of pain erupting from her throat that brought her back, she didn't know. She only knew that the blood dripping from her arm was more a disappointment than surprise.

She glanced around, her fear that someone had seen what she did, causing her to move with haste. Luckily the cut was just above her wrist. She pulled a tissue from her pocket, held it to the wound and secured it with her glove, then began gathering up what pieces of the broken glass she could find. After hurrying to the nearest trash can to dump the evidence, she backtracked and with a few quick scoops, covered the red drops with fresh snow.

Her goal now was to get away from town before anyone saw her, but just in case someone did, she knew not to appear flustered or in a hurry. So, instead of skirting the park, Grace chose to once again take the longer route and meander through it, only this time she would check out the arched bridge on her way through; a bridge that according to Charlie sat dead center of the park, and also marked the center point of the Town of St. Thaddaeus itself. That was why the paved paths had been designed as they were, Charlie had told her, to lead you in whichever direction you needed to go.

As Grace reached the start of the nearest intersecting sidewalk, she spotted a small plaque beneath a tree. It read:

You are entering Gabriel Path.
As ruling angel of the west,
Gabriel offers clarity and insight.
Let not the westerly wind blow you astray
but allow its gentle breeze to guide
you to where you should be.

Grace recalled the time she'd questioned Father Tim about a statue placed in a courtyard adjacent to the rectory. She was maybe nine at the time, and Father had explained that the statue beheld the image of Ariel, the angel of protection. He'd assured Grace that whether she believed or not, "Angels are forever all around us, and when you truly have a need, the one who can help you the most will be there."

Grace hadn't believed in angels then any more than she did today, and yet, the farther she traversed the winding path, the warmer, more comforted she felt. It was as if Father Tim himself had wrapped his arms around her in protection, just as he did each time she visited.

Before long, Grace came to the arched bridge. Here, the separate paths met before ambling off in the four cardinal directions.

As Grace climbed, the clump of her boot heels against the wooden slats echoed in the crisp, cold air. She neared the highest point of the bridge, and an overwhelming desire to take a minute and admire the amazing view struck her.

With her elbows braced on the railing, she ignored the twinge of pain in her wrist, sucked in a deep breath, and looked down into the half-frozen river, then out to the landscape and vast never-ending fields of evergreens visible in every direction. But as her attention shifted to the majestic snow-covered mountain range to the west and the colorful sky overhead, from the corner of her eye, something moved.

Grace barely managed to hold in a gasp.

With a twist in that direction, she saw a brooding figure sitting on the floor of the bridge, his feet dangling over the side, and the railing at his back. *He must have been there all along, but how could I have not seen him?*

More importantly, was he contemplating jumping? she wondered. Judging by the lopsided grin on his face as he turned to stare at her from over his shoulder, Grace didn't think so.

Over the next minute or longer, the man offered no greeting. He just sat there and stared at her as she stared at him in return, neither saying a word to the other. Meanwhile, a myriad of conflicting thoughts and emotions whirled through Grace's head.

She should leave at once; he could be dangerous, lurking, just waiting for someone like her to come by. He could be as alone as she, as fragile and vulnerable. She tried to discern which by his expression or what she saw in his eyes, but both were unreadable.

He looked to be in his mid-thirties, she mused, give or take a year or three, his brown hair a little long in her estimation, yet his mustache and goatee neatly trimmed.

There was something about him, Grace thought with a downward curve of her mouth. He looked dark, dangerous, and disreputable, although she did tend to let her imagination run amok at times, and she would hate to walk away thinking she'd misjudged him.

After a long, uncomfortable stretch of time, she decided to break the silence. "What are you staring at?" Grace asked with an attempt to add a defiant tone to her shaky voice.

"You."

The single syllable came out like a rusty croak. Grace wanted to run—that's what instinct told her to do—but to show fear openly was more than just a little unwise. Another lesson she'd learned early in life. So even though every muscle in her body tensed with abject cowardice, Grace held her ground.

She didn't relish the idea of turning her back on the man, either— she knew well what it was like to be alone in the world—but to avoid that assessing gaze, she shrugged and returned her focus to the view.

"I don't recall seeing you around here before," he said. "You're new in town?"

Grace hesitated before turning back to face him. "Yes, but only temporarily."

"Why's that?"

"Why temporarily?" He nodded, and Grace shrugged again. "Self-preservation, I guess you could say."

"Care to elaborate?" he asked with a sarcastic chuckle.

Grace couldn't fathom why she'd admitted that, so all she said was, "Not particularly."

He nodded as if he understood. "Well, any new resident that isn't under the age of fifteen or over the age of fifty is a welcome sight in this town. And one that's as hot as you are...? Baby, it'll be a damn shame if someone doesn't change your mind about moving on."

Grace chose not to acknowledge what she was sure he considered a compliment.

The man's smile—if you could call it that—wasn't exactly leering, but his last comment, along with his presence, had effectively busted her serene bubble. She pushed away from the railing and started forward.

"Wait!" The stranger swung his legs up onto the bridge and got to his feet, his abrupt movements causing Grace to freeze for a heartbeat or two before taking a quick step in reverse.

She saw now that he was of average height and lean. He wore blue jeans, black boots and a black leather jacket over a faded t-shirt.

Not so dangerous looking after all, although he did have that young Johnny Depp thing going. Still, there was something about him that urged her to give him the benefit of her doubt.

"Why are you running off?" he asked. "I didn't get the impression you were in a hurry earlier."

Fearing any sudden movement on her part would prove her instincts wrong and cause him to pounce, Grace stayed where she was. A tremor of unease began to grow inside her; a feeling she knew was likely misplaced, but couldn't seem to convince herself was true.

On the other hand, there was a note of desperation in his voice that had Grace wondering again why she had found him sitting alone on the edge of a bridge with his feet dangling over an icy river.

She licked her lips. "What do you want?"

"Just someone to talk to. You can spare five minutes, can't you?"

The underlying plea in his tone had thickened, and as much as Grace wanted to ignore it, she found she couldn't. Perhaps he too had spent Thanksgiving alone, she thought, although not by choice.

Having learned to be cautious in all things, Grace put some distance between them before giving him those five minutes. She moved to the opposite side of the bridge, leaned back against the railing and crossed her arms over her middle, then waited for him to start the conversation.

Appearing to understand, the man took up a similar pose by leaning back with his elbows braced on the opposite rail and his ankles crossed. The stance might have been casual, Grace mused, but the neediness still shown in his eyes.

"People around here call me Hank."

"Grace," she replied with a stiff nod.

"Where you from, Grace?"

"Here and there."

"So nowhere in particular. Did you move to St. Thad with family?"

"No."

"Just my luck," he said with a sigh and shake of his head. "I finally have someone to talk to, and she can barely speak in full sentences."

"Look." Grace straightened away from the railing. "I'm not up for playing Twenty Questions, so if you don't mind—"

"No, wait. Just hold on a minute," Hank nearly sputtered as he lurched forward a step. "Okay, I'll stop with the questions. Questions about you that is, but...can you tell me what day it is?"

Grace narrowed her eyes.

"No, I'm serious," he said with a snort of laughter. "See, you're the first person I've laid eyes on since sun up, so I'm thinking today must be some kind of holiday."

"You're saying you don't know that today is Thanksgiving?"

His mouth quirked. "Lost track of time, I guess."

Hank started toward her at a lazy pace sending Grace into a panic. "Stay where you are," she ordered with her palms flung out in front of her. "Please."

Hank froze. Grace interpreted the expression on his face as part confusion, part amusement, and couldn't blame him for either sentiment. She knew she was acting irrationally, knew he hadn't said or done anything threatening, and her brain acknowledged that he'd stopped advancing toward her when she'd asked, but still, her heart continued to race.

After giving herself a stern lecture, she dropped her hands. "I'm sorry. I don't know why I—"

"Don't apologize, you'll ruin the moment. Besides, I can see I make you nervous, and even though I'm curious to know why, I'm not asking. I won't move from this spot, either, I swear."

The heat of embarrassment crawled over her exposed cheeks, and as Grace searched for words, the shouts of children at play came from somewhere not too far in the distance. She turned to see who was coming and watched as the Haney twins—she recognized them now—reached the foot of the bridge before stopping to catch their breath.

That's what she assumed they were doing, at nay rate, until both twisted to look back in the direction from which they'd come and began shouting taunts to someone lagging behind.

"I win, I win," the girl chanted.

"No, I win," the boy argued.

Grace followed the direction of the children's gazes and spotted the top of a chestnut-brown head coming over the rise. Seconds later, the figure of a man came into full view but enchanted by the children as she was, his looming presence didn't immediately register.

She looked on as the twins laughed and cheered while waiting for their companion to catch up, and just as he did, Grace turned back to Hank, an excuse as to why she had to leave hovering on her lips.

But Hank was gone.

CHAPTER 6

Odd, she thought, that Hank would leave now when he was so obviously desperate for company, and here, more had just arrived.

With an inward shrug and one last glance at the twins, Grace started for the far end of the bridge. She got no more than a few steps beyond where she'd been, however, before a sound like rumbling thunder gathered behind her, the bridge's wooden slats trembling beneath her feet. A moment later, a small hand tugged at her coat sleeve.

"Hi!" It was the girl, Grace saw, as she looked down to see gray-green eyes and a huge smile staring up at her.

"Hello."

"I know you," the little girl announced.

"Me too," the boy chimed in as he skidded to a halt. "You work at the dog book store."

"Barker's Books," a male voice corrected. Apparently, in no hurry, the man accompanying the children approached at a more sedate speed.

This man was tall, or taller than Hank at any rate. Wide-shouldered, narrowed-hipped, and better than average-looking with chestnut-brown hair that curled at its tips. The shadow of stubble covering his face added to his appeal rather than detracted. It emphasized the masculine shape of his jaw and lent a hint of toughness to an otherwise gentle veneer. Then again, the thin lips and straight, narrow brows spoke of knowledge. An understanding of the harshness life had to offer, and an unwillingness to accept it.

He had an amused look in his caramel-colored eyes as he nodded in greeting. Eyes that it took Grace a moment to realize she recognized. This was the man she'd encountered when she first pulled into town.

Grace gave him a brisk nod in reply, then turned her attention to the child now tugging on the hem of her coat.

"You know me, too. I'm Alec, 'member?"

"I'm Ainsley," the girl added, vying for equal attention. "You 'member us. Nanna bringed us to the dog book store, and you read us a story 'cause Mister Charlie had a 'pointment to get his teeth pulled out."

"Nanna says she hopes Mister Charlie has a 'pointment next time too," Alec informed her, "'cause you read better."

The girl—Ainsley, Grace corrected herself—turned to the man accompanying them. "She does the voices really funny. You have to come with us next time so you can see."

The man chuckled. "According to Nanna, I should come with you every time to make sure you behave."

Grace assumed their father was referring to yesterday's incident. Although Ainsley had eyes that were sometimes more green than gray, where her brother's were a vivid blue, and the shape of their faces not quite the same—Alec's a little more square, Ainsley's more oval—there was no mistaking they were twins. She guessed their age to be close to five, and under Mrs. Haney's charge, they were an industrious pair, yesterday's antics being a perfect example.

As Grace understood it, Ainsley had decided a bit of rearranging was in order and began by emptying a red wagon that sat in the children's section loaded with everything from Dr. Seuss to Judy Blume. Before anyone was the wiser, she and her brother then refilled the wagon with as many Christmas books as it could hold, and while encouraging bystanders—namely the Pulaski boys—cheered them on, the pair pulled the wagon to the front of the store, where according to an eager seven-year-old stool pigeon (a/k/a Jordan Pulaski) they dumped the contents of the loaded wagon onto the floor.

With the wagon then parked next to a display table holding boxed Christmas cards, the twins proceeded to shove the cards over the side. Grace had to give them credit for that as a fair amount of the boxes did, in fact, land in the wagon as they had proclaimed was their intention.

From what Grace garnered through a whispered conversation or two later that afternoon, up until the sound of tumbling boxes gained everyone's attention, the children's Nana had been too busy admiring the latest arrival of paperbacks with Scottish hunks adorning their covers to keep an eye on her charges.

It wasn't funny at the time, not to Lizbeth Haney at any rate, but remembering it now, Grace couldn't hold back her amusement. A nervous giggle escaped before she could stifle it.

Their father raised his brows. "I take it you witnessed Ainsley's budding organizational skills."

If not for the twins' presence, Grace would have already made her escape, but there was something about these two, and perhaps their father, as well, she begrudgingly admitted, that put her at ease. Maybe it was simply because she had only minutes earlier given herself such a thorough lecture, reminding herself that she was out in the open, out where she had room to run if the need arose.

She expelled a held breath. "To be fair, I believe Alec was just as involved. At least, that's how Jordan Pulaski tells it."

The man shrugged. "Ainsley was the instigator, I have no doubt. Alec just goes along with her."

"What's a *inst*-gator?"

He looked down, patted the little girl on the head, and winked. "You are."

Then he smiled and held out a hand to Grace. "Colin Haney. Nice to meet you."

"Um, Grace. Grace St. John." She didn't acknowledge his offered hand but instead placed both of hers on the children's heads while doing her best to keep from meeting the man's gaze.

"We had turkey dinner at Nana and Pop's house," Alec informed her. "Now we're going home for ice cream 'cause Nana's had enough of us for one day. Are you going home for ice cream, too?"

"Not hardly," Grace replied with an exaggerated shiver. "It's too cold for ice cream."

"Nuh-uh," both children exclaimed in unison. "It's never too cold for ice cream."

It was then that Grace noticed the drop in temperature. The sky had gone from pinks and oranges to more purples and indigo blue, and the lamps illuminating the paved paths had come on. She rubbed her arms and dared a glance at the twin's father, who she found watching her with a somewhat assessing look in his eyes, not unlike the way he had that first day while giving directions.

She wasn't sure how to take the scrutiny. Didn't the man have a wife? And if so, where was she? Then again, Grace allowed, perhaps she was misinterpreting those stares. Maybe it wasn't interest she saw in his eyes but simple curiosity.

Taking it for the former, Grace wanted to be repelled by his interest. Even expected to be. Instead, she experienced something akin to a long sip of hot chocolate on a cold night.

Stupid. Stupid, stupid.

"Well," she began around a lump in her throat, "I'm sure you want to get these two home, and I really have to go, so... Enjoy what's left of your evening."

With a quick smile that was in no way genuine and a wave to the children, Grace turned and hurried across the bridge, fighting herself not to break into a sprint.

41

CHAPTER 7

"Charlie always has the best ideas to boost holiday sales," Allie praised from her post behind their one and only cash register. Beside her, Grace plopped down another armload of holiday shopping bags, as the first batch had flown out the door at record-breaking speed.

Grace rubbed stiff fingers over her lower back. "I don't know what he's done in the past, but I can certainly attest to this year's Black Friday being a hit. I haven't stopped moving since we opened."

Bowing her head, she added, "Which explains why Charlie didn't fire me after—"

"Grace, stop it!" Allie whispered, her tone harsh. "Quit dwelling on what happened with Zee this morning. That was nothing more than one of those unfortunate events we'll be laughing about come tomorrow, and besides, it was more my fault than yours. I'm the one who unlocked the front door without telling you, and I'm the one who told Zee his Santa suit was in the storeroom. If Charlie should fire anyone, it's me."

"Don't be ridiculous."

"No more ridiculous than you're being." Allie greeted the next customer in line and began tallying the man's purchases, while Grace slipped them into a shopping bag, her frown just as pronounced as it had been all morning. She couldn't help but metaphorically continue to kick herself for having overreacted as she did.

As Allie handed the customer his receipt, she leaned close so only Grace could hear. "I guarantee Charlie's forgotten all about it by now, and I wish to God you'd do the same because every time you bring it up, I feel even more guilty than I did when it happened. Now, I don't want to hear another word."

Grace winced and nodded. Allie was right; there was no sense in dwelling on it. After all, Charlie had saved her from herself by coming in behind Zee before she could do the man any real harm. And how could she hold it against Zee for seeing right through her from the start, in any case? He knew as well as she did that she didn't belong here.

Reversing the subject back to what they had been speaking about earlier, Grace asked, "So, where are all these customers coming from, anyway? They can't all live in St. Thad."

"Oh, as long as the weather's accommodating, we'll get carloads from neighboring towns this time of year. Most people don't care to drive all the way to Steamboat Springs or Silverthorne if they don't have to, and Denver's an overnight trip if you're going to do it right, which a lot of people just can't afford."

Grace glanced at the time and saw it was nearing two o'clock. Allie had only just returned from her lunch break, and Grace had yet to take hers as she was in charge of the children's section, and the place had been a veritable madhouse since Charlie unlocked the doors at nine.

Was that really only five *hours ago*? Grace thought with a groan.

Looking around, she noted that the number of customers crowded into the store had finally dwindled, although not by much, and no one seemed to mind the wait to check out; everyone seemed to be in good spirits as they laughed and chatted with neighbors or took advantage of the wait to peruse their soon-to-be purchases.

Part of Charlie's Black Friday lure was that Barker's Books hosted the town's one and only live Santa Claus. Needless to say, the children's section had to be expanded to allow room for Santa and his elves, not to mention Charlie's English sheepdog, Barker, also present and accounted for in all his shaggy-haired splendor. Barker was presenting each boy and girl who came in—while supplies lasted—with their very own copy of *How Barker Almost Ruined Christmas*, a story Charlie wrote himself.

"Well, you should take your break while you can," Allie warned. "This is probably as quiet as it's going to get between now and closing."

Half-listening, Grace stood on tip-toe as she strained to see over the heads of customers milling about. She scanned the area looking for her unaccounted-for boss and spotted the Pulaski boys running amok around Santa's empty chair, and upon further survey, Lizbeth Haney with her nose stuck in a paperback a few feet away.

Grace wondered if that meant the Haney twins were here as well.

"You're right," Grace said, stretching a little higher. "And I still need to run that errand. The house I rented is starting to reek of dirty dishwater, and I don't know what's clogging the drain, but the smell makes me think *dead body*." The moment those last two words came out of her mouth, Grace wanted to snatch them back. She glanced around to see who else might have heard, and, peeking out from over the top of her paperback, Mrs. Haney exchanged a look with Allie, which Grace caught. Her gaze moved from one to the other, but Mrs. Haney didn't look up again, and Allie started to fidget under the scrutiny before choking on a laugh.

"If you're telling me you know what a dead body smells like," Allie said with amusement in her tone, "girl, we need to talk."

Allie thanked another customer and greeted the next who happened to be the same woman Grace had met on the sidewalk that first evening.

The cheerful woman winked as she laid her purchases on the counter then leaned close as if imparting a secret. "The Lord knows how much it pleases me to see you here, Grace, and everyone else feels the same, so don't you go letting old memories reach out and snatch a good day away—He's got good things waitin' for you, and they're right around the corner."

Unsure how to respond, and finding it hard to believe her thoughts had been so clearly visible on her face, Grace kept her mouth shut as she wrapped and bagged the woman's purchases.

Allie nudged Grace with her hip recalling her attention, and speaking just a little too loudly, she said, "In any case, I forgot about you needing to get to the hardware store. You should have taken your break the same time Santa did."

"You're probably right about that, too," Grace replied, her gaze shooting to the far corner where a gold-painted chair stood center stage.

She wasn't about to admit to Allie, or anyone for that matter, her real problem with Zee. After all, how could she admit to being afraid the man knew who she really was? Or more precisely, that he knew the dark secrets she hid inside?

Grace held back a shudder and put a smile on her face. "You have to admit, though, if I take my lunch break *after* Santa returns from feeding his reindeer, I get that much more of a reprieve from his disapproving sneers. So, if I can find Charlie and he can fill in for me..."

CHAPTER 8

"Why on God's green earth would you put that woman in charge of innocent children?" Zee wanted to know.

"Her name is Grace," Charlie reminded his friend, "and I put her in charge of the kids because she's good with them."

"Is that so? Well, she ain't good with anyone over twelve, is she?"

Zee's break was just about up, so using the mirror that hung on the back of the closed door to the storeroom, he once again donned the white beard and adjusted his droopy red hat.

Despite his good friend arguing the point every blasted year, Charlie suspected Zee secretly enjoyed playing Santa. Although Charlie would gladly play the role himself, his swarthy skin, black hair and matching mustache would give him away in a heartbeat. Zee, on the other hand, was the best choice they had. He was of average height and had a full head of snow-white hair. He also had the beginnings of a potbelly, which Charlie enhanced to Santa Claus proportions by supplying a good amount of padding, along with the red suit.

From his perch on the corner of the desk, one leg swinging over the side, Charlie studied Zee's reflection in the looking glass. "I've never seen you so opposed to anyone before. What's up with that?"

Zee grumbled something under his breath, then said, "Not everyone's suited to small towns, as you well know, and I could tell right off that woman doesn't belong here."

Charlie sighed. "Duncan says he likes Grace just fine. As does Virginia, Mac, and Allie too."

"Good for them."

Charlie shook his head. "Something tells me this foul mood of yours has a lot to do with what happened this morning. You wanna explain to me again why I found Grace defending herself with a five hundred page hardcover when I walked in?"

Zee bowed his head. "All I did was come looking for this Claus get-up you've got me wearing for the umpteenth year in a row, and just because I stuck my head in the storeroom before you'd officially opened for business, that woman took my head off!"

Charlie chuckled while his friend lowered his weight onto the only chair in the cramped space to pull on a pair of black plastic boots.

"You go ahead and laugh," Zee said with a sneer, "but I'm telling you, that woman doesn't belong in the customer service industry. Mark my words, she's going to put a damper on sales."

"There you go exaggerating again."

An incredulous scowl took over Zee's timeworn face. "Exaggerate, you say? Charlie, that woman called me a dirty old man! She accused me of–of– Well, I can't even say it out loud, but I'll tell you this, I didn't like it one bit."

"So you startled her, and she overreacted. Get over it. And dammit, Zee, her name is Grace, not 'that woman.'"

"I don't care what her name is. No one's going to accuse me of being a crotchety old lecher."

"Well, she got the old and crotchety part right," Charlie mumbled, managing to get a reluctant snort of laughter in response.

"We have to remember," Charlie continued, "the girl isn't used to how we do things around here, everyone coming and going as they please. Why, just think about all the bad things that happen nowadays to single females, and especially in those big cities. That's what she's accustomed to having to worry about."

Zee grumbled something under his breath Charlie couldn't make out, then asked, "Where'd she come from, anyway?"

"According to her references, Grace has lived in a number of places in the past several years, all of them big cities. Denver most recent, where she managed the children's department in one of those big chain stores. Did a fine job of it, too, according to her manager."

"So why she'd leave?"

Charlie shook his head. "Seems Grace doesn't stay put very long."

"Doesn't surprise me none," Zee jeered as he slipped his arms into the top half of the Santa suit. "Sounds reliable, don't she?"

"I won't have you bad-mouthing my new employee," Charlie said, pointing a stiff finger in the direction of his old friend's chest. "Sure, Grace is cautious, maybe even a little leery of strangers. Men, in particular, from what I can tell. But you've seen for yourself how great she is with those kids, Zee, and doesn't it make you wonder?"

"Wonder what?"

"Don't be dense. A lot of lost souls have found their way to St. Thad for one reason or another over the years and seems to me, Grace is one more."

"Yeah, so, what are we supposed to do about it?"

"Help her is what."

"Help her? And how do you propose to do that when the woman won't let anyone get close enough to find out what her problem is?"

Charlie waved a dismissive hand in the air. "You just got off on a bad foot with her is all. I know Grace comes off a little standoffish—"

"'Standoffish' my patooty. She's cold and abrupt and...shifty."

"'*Shifty?*'"

"Yeah, shifty. That woman's hiding something, mark my words."

"Finally, something we can agree on."

CHAPTER 9

She found the twins lying on the floor, their chins propped in the palms of their hands, their faces in a book. They looked so sweet and innocent, Grace had to wonder why she ever expected to find them in the midst of some sort of mischief.

Santa had yet to return to his post—she was happy to see—and Charlie was nowhere in sight, so Grace sat down at the child-sized table, leaned forward, and peered over Alec's shoulder.

"'Green Eggs and Ham'," she read. "Sounds kind of yucky if you ask me."

Alec turned his face up to hers with the most beatific smile Grace had ever witnessed. Next to him, Ainsley rolled over and showed her dimples.

"Nana maked us green eggs," the girl said. "I liked it, but Alec frowed up."

"Double yuck!" Grace scrunched up her face sending both children into a fit of giggles.

A short time later, and halfway through *Horton Hears a Who,* another favored Dr. Seuss, Charlie came up behind them. "Uh, Grace, Allie reminded me that you haven't taken a lunch break yet."

"Oh. No, I..." A flush of guilt heated Grace's cheeks as she snapped the book closed and looked up at her employer. "I was looking for you to see if now would be a good time, but then I let myself get distracted by these two. Sorry."

Charlie grinned at the two unrepentant faces. "Now's perfect. You take all the time you need, Grace."

"Thanks," she said while unfolding herself from the child-sized chair. "I won't be long. I just need to run by the hardware store, then I'll grab some takeout at Dewley's Diner and come right back."

"The hardware store, you say?" Charlie tapped his chin with a blunt finger. "Hey, since you're going that way, would you mind taking these two kiddos with you and leaving them with their uncle? Lizbeth offered to stick around and assist Santa for the remainder of the afternoon, which'll be a tremendous help, especially while you're gone. But she was going to have to deliver the kiddos first, and I don't want you waiting any longer to take that break. Plus, if you're going that way, anyhow..."

Grace glanced down at the twins who were already bouncing with excitement at the prospect. "Please, please," they shouted in unison.

"You want *me* to take them?"

"It sure would help," Charlie replied. "You don't mind, do you?"

Yes, yes, I absolutely do! her inner voice screamed. Out loud, she said, "Well, no, but... What about their mother? Can't she—"

"We don't have one," Ainsley put in.

"We got a mom," Alec argued. "She just got lost." He turned his cherub face up to Grace's, his stunning turquoise eyes filled with an innocence only the very young could possess.

Grace struggled to speak. "I suppose I could if Mrs. Haney feels all right entrusting them to me."

Whatever reply Charlie had planned wasn't necessary as Lizbeth came bustling over at that exact moment. "Oh, Grace, I'm so glad we caught you. Allie mentioned that you were running over to the hardware store and I wanted to ask—

"I just did," Charlie interrupted, "and Grace says she'll be happy to take the twins with her."

"Wonderful!" Lizbeth exclaimed, clapping her hands together. "Ainsley. Alec. I'll bet you two can show Grace the way."

****

Uncle, Uncle!" the twins called out in unison as they nearly knocked him over.

Colin blinked in surprise. Not that he hadn't expected them because he had. But his mother promised to drop the twins off by three, and that's where the surprise came in. It wasn't his mother he saw step inside behind the pair, but St. Thad's newest resident, the cautious and wholesomely pretty Grace St. John.

Recalling the not-so-subtle remarks made by his parents over the Thanksgiving dinner table, Colin suspected a bit of matchmaking was in the works, and couldn't say he minded one bit.

"She has an innocent look about her that reminds me of a meadow covered in new-fallen snow," his dad had said, *"with the complexion of an angel and the sparkle of moon dust in her eyes."* While his mother had been sure to tell him that Grace had traveled to St. Thad all on her own, a fact which Colin already knew for himself.

He surveyed the woman standing in his doorway and had to admit that although Grace wasn't what most would consider a perfect beauty, he wholeheartedly agreed with his father's assessment.

Her nose could be construed by some as just a tad too wide, her chin on the verge of pointy with a hint of an indentation that spoke of stubbornness.

None of which should be considered a flaw in Colin's estimation.

Not when paired with an incredibly lush mouth, thick, honey-blonde hair, and luminous skin as smooth and pale as vanilla cream.

He wanted to devour her.

She also had the saddest eyes he had ever seen; bottle-green with flecks of silver that tore at his heart every time he looked into them.

Each time he saw her, his initial reaction was like a sucker punch in the gut. She probably thought him slow-witted, but once he recovered from the initial blow—which took less than a minute—an unexplainable need to gather her in and never let go would swamp him.

Unfortunately for Grace, the wicked side of him inevitably followed those feelings with an overwhelming desire to tease and torment in the best of ways. The former Colin hadn't dared to attempt. As for the latter, well, on the previous two occasions they'd met, he held his true nature in check as best he could. After all, she was no more than a stranger passing through on their first encounter, and on the second, not as slow-witted as he might have appeared, he had sensed she was as nervous as a cat caught between two rocking chairs.

Just now, though, if he wasn't mistaken—and Colin didn't think he was considering Grace hadn't taken more than one step inside the front door—the woman was either nervous or repelled by him. Hell, maybe he had bad breath.

Nah.

More likely, she was worried he'd be upset about the mid-afternoon treat he spied remnants of on the twin's faces.

Turning his attention where it belonged, Colin got down on his haunches and gathered the twins in a noisy bear hug while Grace continued to hover near the door.

"Just how did you two get here, I wonder?"

"We bringed Grace all the way from the dog book store," Alec explained, "and we didn't get lost even once."

"Is that so?" With narrowed eyes, Colin leaned in and gave a corner of Ainsley's mouth a lick sending her into a rapture of giggles. "You must have made a detour then because LuAnn's is in the other direction."

"We told her you'd want us to bringed you some ice cream, too," Ainsley exclaimed, "but Grace said we first gotta find out what flavor."

"She did, did she?"

Ainsley nodded, her expression serious, her eyes full of mischief.

"And what did you tell her?"

"I told her you like pink 'cause it's sweet like little girls are 'posed to be."

"I telled her you like chocolate with nuts in it," Alec interjected.

Colin laughed and brushed his hand through Alec's thick head of hair. "I like them both, buddy, especially if you add nuts."

"See?" Alec shouted as he ran over to latch onto one of Grace's hands and pull her forward. "I told you Uncle likes nuts in it. Can we go back now and get him some?"

Grace had yet to move or say a word since stepping through the door. Colin waved a hand in front of her face. "Yo. Earth to Grace."

She blinked. "You're their uncle?"

"That's me. Uncle Colin."

Alec tugged on the hem of Grace's winter coat, reminding her she had yet to answer his question.

"Um... I'm sorry, Alec, I can't. I've got to get back to work."

"But, you didn't have ice cream yet."

Grace snuffled a laugh. "Yes, and I told you that's because I need to have my lunch first."

"Uncle gets us lunch at Dewley's sometimes," Ainsley added. "He can get you some, too, and when you're full, we can get more ice cream."

Colin was just about to add a little coaxing of his own when Grace lifted her gaze in his direction, and the hint of panic he saw in those sad green eyes stopped him.

"Hey," he said, turning to the twins, "why don't you two go on back and get Grace a licorice stick to hold her over until she has time to eat?" The two raced out of sight with cheers of glee echoing in their wake.

Grace cleared her throat. "I thought you were their father."

Colin shrugged. "Well, I'm not, but I am their guardian, at least until their dad returns. Whenever the hell that might be," he said, adding those last few words from under his breath. To Colin's relief, Grace didn't appear to have heard.

"Your mother said it would be okay to stop for ice cream," Grace began before he had a chance to speak again. "I hope you don't—"

"Mind?" he finished for her. "Not at all. I appreciate you spending time with them."

"She was coming anyway," Ainsley chimed in as she came to a sliding halt a foot in front of Grace with the offer of a handful of red licorice sticks, and her brother right behind her.

Colin had to swallow his disappointment. He'd hoped to have more than ten seconds alone with Grace, but the twins were faster than he'd anticipated. He rubbed a hand over Ainsley's head, following the length of her hair and finishing with a slight tug on the ends.

"Was she?" he asked without taking his eyes off the woman in question. But not one of the three replied, particularly not Grace, who, if he wasn't mistaken, kept her focus on the twins with purposeful intent. Colin leaned a hip against the counter and waited.

Grace looked up at him a long moment later, and again, Colin lost every ounce of breath in his lungs.

Then he saw a shift. A change he noted first in those fascinating green eyes as if a barrier had been lifted. Her lips parted emitting a soft sigh, and she visibly relaxed, even if only to the slightest degree.

Her gaze still focused on the twins, Grace began, "The house I've rented—"

"You didn't like the B&B?" he interrupted.

She looked up, allowing her gaze to meet his. "It's not that. I spent a night there, and thank you for the recommendation by the way, but since I decided to stay for a while, I needed something more private, and Duncan—your father, that is—told me about this house—"

"The old Cambroto place out on Maple. I heard."

"Right. Well, Duncan took me over to see the place and—

"And you still thought it would be a good idea to rent it?"

Grace huffed out a breath. "It's perfectly fine. At least, I thought so until—"

"That place hasn't been given much attention since Florence's dad passed away. Probably a lot of things that could use some repair." Colin struggled to hide his amusement—she was easier to provoke than he'd anticipated—as he interrupted again.

"I'm realizing that now, which is why—"

"I hope Florence had that roof inspected. More than two inches of snow and the ceiling might come down on your head."

"Actually—"

"That's not what happened, is it?"

Grace's lips thinned, confirming Colin's suspicion that she'd hit her limit with his shenanigans.

He hid his grin by looking down at the two faces who stood on either side of him looking back, both with licorice sticks hanging from between their lips. Alec appeared to be oblivious as to his uncle's true plan, while Ainsley, he could tell, knew precisely what he hoped to accomplish. A dimple in her cheek winked with delight.

"The kitchen sink is backed up," Grace blurted out.

A corner of Colin's mouth lifted. "That should be an easy fix. Have you tried—"

"I tried a plunger," she interrupted, giving him a bit of his own medicine. "It didn't help, so I thought maybe some of that liquid stuff would work."

"Ah. Well, I can sell you some, but if a plunger didn't work, I'm not sure it would do you any good. How about a snake?"

Grace gave him a puzzled look.

He held up a finger, walked a few aisles away to pull a flexible plumber's snake from a shelve, and waved it in the air.

"Oh. Right," she said. "That kind of snake. How do you use it?"

Colin lifted a brow. "I take it household repairs isn't your forte?"

"I'm sure I can manage. If you'll just—"

"The plumbing in that place has to be more than a hundred and fifty years old. You'd probably be better off calling a handyman, and I'm sure that's what your landlord would want."

Grace nibbled on her bottom lip, a gesture Colin found incredibly arousing. He wanted to suck on that generous lip and—

"Florence did say if I had any problems I was to call Duncan..." she mused aloud.

"Exactly. Haney's Plumbing at your service."

Grace blinked. "Duncan's the town plumber?"

"Not precisely. But if there's a household repair that needs doing, Haney's Hardware and Appliances is the place to find the help you need. Why don't I follow you home?"

"Can we come and watch?" Ainsley asked, bouncing on her toes.

"Yeah, and we'll bringed ice cream!" Alec exclaimed.

Grace shifted her weight from one foot to the other before giving the twins her attention. "I won't be home until well after your bedtime, I'm afraid." She switched her gaze to Colin. "I'd like to give that liquid stuff a try, please."

"Suit yourself." With a shrug, he pulled a bottle from a nearby shelf, then slid behind the counter to ring up her purchase. "You change your mind, or this doesn't do the job, just give the store a call. Either Pop or I can come right over."

Grace nodded in reply but failed to look him in the eye, giving Colin the distinct impression she had no intention of calling whether she needed help or not.

CHAPTER 10

While hiding a self-satisfied grin behind the rim of her cup of hot cocoa, Mary Francis listened intently to the morning's gossip at Dewley's Diner.

Everything was humming along as planned. Grace had accepted the job at the bookstore, moved into the old Cambroto place, and whether the girl knew it or not, she was making friends. Folks liked her, and even though Grace wouldn't admit it, she liked them too.

And although the girl was known to move on without a second's hesitation, Mary Francis believed Grace St. John's sense of commitment would buy them the time needed to get the poor girl's life on the track it was meant to be traveling.

Of course, Mary Francis wasn't *that* sure of Grace, especially when she thought of the way the girl had picked up and skedaddled out of Denver without a by-your-leave. It was all there in the report Mary Francis received when she accepted this blessed assignment, and she was determined to see that Grace found what she was searching for. Even if the obtuse child didn't know she was.

And whether Grace believed or not.

Which meant Mary Francis still had *a lot* of work to do and an uncertain time frame in which to get it done.

Among the dozen or so customers in the diner, more than half were even now discussing the town's newest resident in some form or another. But the conversation Mary Francis zeroed in on was the one between Virginia, who had arrived only minutes before with her daily delivery of baked goods, her niece Mackenzie, and Dewley the diner's owner, cook, and consummate busybody.

Perched on a stool at the counter, Mackenzie savored the last of her breakfast—two eggs over easy and a slice of toast—before heading off to open the gas station. With the heavy snowfall that brought Grace into their town long behind them, Mac had been able to sleep in this morning and was only now starting her day.

Dewley folded his elbows over the faded countertop. "I don't expect Colin'll be thanking Lizbeth for matchmaking like that, but what I want to know is, did it work?"

"Not so far as Duncan tells it," Virginia replied. "But you can get only so much information out of a pair of five-year-olds."

Mac shook her head in disgust. "You all need to leave Grace be. The woman made it clear from day one she wanted her privacy."

"Oh, please," Virginia said, waving the comment away. "That girl's aura is begging for someone to butt in. Plus, any decent soul with a head on their shoulders can see Grace needs some stability in her life."

Mac scoffed. "And Colin Haney's the one who's going to give it to her?"

"Now, hold on you two," Dewley cut in. "Before you get going again, keep in mind that it's Duncan and Lizbeth themselves who started that campaign."

"Only because Duncan's good buddy Zee is so against Grace even being here," Mac argued.

"If you ask me, that's why Duncan's all the more determined to prove Grace belongs in St. Thad just as much as any one of us does."

"Yeah, well, I'd like to prove that old geezer wrong just as much as the next guy, but not at Colin's expense. He's got enough on his plate. Besides that, not one of you knows the first thing about where Grace came from or what brought her here."

Virginia laid a gentle hand on her niece's arm and gave it a soothing pat. "I know how close you and Colin have always been,

58

Mackenzie, but it's time to face facts—the man isn't interested in you that way."

Mac nearly choked on a mouthful of toast. "I never said—"

"Don't worry. I'm pretty sure he's oblivious, so there's no need to be embarrassed."

Mac rolled her eyes, and Virginia kept talking. "I'm even more sure that whatever's hiding in Grace's past, it's nothing to do with breaking the law. Not by her doing."

"What makes you so sure?"

Virginia turned to her niece with a slackened jaw. "I thought you liked the girl?"

"I did. I do," Mac corrected. "I'm just saying, we don't know the first thing about her, and you have to admit, a woman her age, traveling to nowhere in particular, and all alone at Christmas time to boot, is pretty odd."

"We do know a little," Dewley said, jumping back in. "I heard from Charlie that just before coming here, Grace had been working at one of those big bookstores over in Denver. He also told me that's just one of a half dozen or so places she's lived in as many years. Someone who moves around that much and that often does leave you wondering."

Mary Francis heard enough. She took one last sip of her hot chocolate, then hurried over and leaned in between the two women to slide both her check and a five-dollar bill across the counter.

As Dewley scooped them both up and headed for the cash register, Mary Francis turned to the women. "Not meanin' to eavesdrop or anythin', but you know, I heard tell that girl not only moves around 'bout as much as a bee flits from flower to flower, but she uses an alias, too!"

Mac blinked. "Are you saying Grace St. John isn't her real name?"

Virginia gasped. "Don't tell me Zee's gone so far as to go snooping on that blasted internet?"

"Oh, well..." Mary Francis began, purposefully stumbling over her words, "I can't rightly say where I heard it."

"Must have been Charlie," Dewley suggested.

"Might have been," Mary Francis confessed with her fingers crossed behind her back. "Or maybe the intel came from that sweet thing, Allie Anne. She's probably gotten to know Grace better than anybody else in town, after all. 'Course, there *was* a lot of supposin' goin' on yesterday over at the beauty salon," she finished with a shameful shake of her head.

"Well, I, for one, don't believe a word of it," Virginia said with a huff.

"Oh, Lordy." Mary Francis wrung her hands. "Last thing I meant to do was upset y'all, and Lord knows I shouldn't be spreadin' unfounded rumors. We all know how people like to make assumptions, and it don't make one bit of never mind if there's truth to it or not."

Mary Francis paused a moment giving their gossiping but well-meaning selves time to think up a whole barnyard full of possibilities before adding, "And who knows? Even if Grace St. John ain't the name the girl was born with, I'll bet there's a good story behind why she's usin' it."

Mary Francis nodded her thanks as Dewley handed over her change, said her goodbyes, and aimed for the door leaving the three behind to put their heads together. From the sidewalk in front of the diner, she slipped on her gloves, glanced heavenward, and winked.

"That'll git some more of them tongues a waggin,'" she whispered to the heavens above. "And with any luck, git us some action."

CHAPTER 11

Colin poked his head into the back office, where his father sat before an old metal desk going over receipts. "Hey, Pop. I'm out of here. You got this?"

"Sure, sure," Duncan said with an absent wave of his hand.

With a nod, Colin headed out, but just before he reached the door, his father came from the back office. "Hey, uh, hold up."

Colin turned with a raised brow. "Sure. Whatcha need?"

"I was wondering..." Duncan rubbed the stubble on his chin. "What are your thoughts on that new filly over at the bookstore? You haven't really said."

Colin snorted a laugh. "If you're referring to Grace, Pop, I don't think she'd appreciate being called a filly."

"No, I'm sure you're right about that," Duncan agreed with a chuckle. "Don't know what got into me."

"Uh-huh. So, why are you asking about Grace?"

"Well. Your mother's got it in her head that you need a woman of your own. And not just because she needs a break from taking care of the twins," Duncan added when Colin winced. "Personally, I agree with her, but even so, I'd rather not park my horse where it isn't welcome. So before I make any attempt at rounding the woman up for you, I'm asking if you're at all interested."

"I'm definitely interested, Pop, but I'm not so sure Grace is."

Duncan clapped his son on the shoulder. "Well, in that case, I'm more than happy to do what I can to see that you two find yourselves in the same corral from time to time so you can get to know one another and see about that. And if she is, well then, the wrangling part I'll leave to you."

Colin shifted his weight and crossed his arms over his chest, all the while trying to hold back a grin. "All right. What have you got in mind?"

Duncan rubbed his hands together. "Well, what I was thinking is this. Let's say I need you to take care of something for me tomorrow after supper. You got any plans?"

Colin shrugged. "So far, my plans involve getting the munchkins fed and put down for the night, then parking myself in front of the TV with a bag of chips and a cold beer to watch the game."

"Okay. We can work with that." Duncan rubbed his chin again. "So, let's say something comes up... Like a household emergency kind of thing, and I don't feel up to playing handyman. Maybe I ate a bad melon or something. Then you'd be available to cover for me, right?"

"Sure. As long as you come and sit with the kids who'll either be asleep or nearly."

"I can do that," Duncan assured him with a nod. "You just get yourself cleaned up and save me a beer. I'll keep your spot warm on that sofa."

Colin didn't bother to hide his amusement or his pleasure. He knew exactly what his father had in mind and was not only more than willing to play along, he was grateful to know he had someone like Duncan Haney in his corner.

"Thanks, Pop."

Duncan winked. "Anytime, Son. Anytime."

CHAPTER 12

Exhausted from a long day at the bookstore, Grace nearly fell into bed, sinking into a deep but restless sleep.

As the sounds that had become all too common of late filled the quiet room, she buried her face in the pillow.

She lay there, her eyes squeezed shut, not moving a muscle or making a sound, afraid to even go so far as to slid the soft pink bear in her arms closer as she heard the slight squeak of a door.

The harsh whispers filled with commands that came next were blocked from her mind with thoughts of a spring breeze blowing through the church courtyard and the statute of an angel looking down upon her head.

The shuffling of sheets and the echoes of a struggle were harder to ignore, as were the whimpers and quiet cries that came after and continued well into the night.

But Grace did as she had always done before. She lay quiet and still, barely allowing herself to breathe as she prayed and thanked God he hadn't yet come for her.

****

Unable to sleep past sun-up, Grace sat in the window of the compact front room, staring out at a sunrise dimmed by fog.

The haunting memories that had filled her dreams the night before continued to replay over and over in her mind until even the simple solitude of a quiet Sunday morning became too loud to bear.

Jumping to her feet, she rushed into her bedroom to dress for church, even though she knew the early morning Mass wouldn't begin for several hours yet.

She tucked her latest letter into a pocket of her winter coat and set out on foot. Walking always helped, whether it was the energy she burnt off or the peace of nature that always seemed to calm her, she wasn't sure; perhaps it was a mixture of both.

Just as Grace hoped, there were no cars on the road this early in the morning and no other citizens of the quaint town of St. Thaddaeus strolling in the chilly morning air. She had the world to herself.

With so much time to spare, Grace figured, if she walked the entire outer path that bordered Araqiel Park, she might just eat up a good hour. However, something pulled at her this morning, and instead, the moment she reached the start of the paved path, she struck out for the bridge at the park's core.

A short time later, the muffled sounds of her footsteps on the damp pavement transformed into the clumping echoes of boot heels as she climbed the wooden bridge.

Once she reached the center, she leaned against the railing and breathed deep. She closed her eyes and listened, hearing only the flap of a bird's wings above, and the calming rush of water over the rocks below. The trickle of melting ice crept in from a few feet away, and next came the friendly chirps of a robin.

Grace stayed just like that for what seemed like forever, her eyes closed, and her body still, listening and allowing the sounds of nature to cleanse the haunting cries from her brain. Then looking out into the icy river, she bit down on the inside of her cheek and willed the memories, the fear, and the pain to all wash away.

What prompted her to glance over to one side at that precise moment she didn't know, but as she did, Grace caught the blur of a familiar leather-clad back disappearing into the trees. Curious, she headed in that same direction.

She didn't call out to him or even try to make her presence known. Instead, she simply followed from a distance, sticking to the pavement, while Hank continued to push his way through plants and brush, saplings and decades' old trees, the sounds of his movements heightened, she assumed, by the rapidly thinning fog.

She paid no attention to where she was going, and no heed to time. And although she still didn't call out, something told her that he knew of her presence and there was no need.

She glanced up at the sky, and with a satisfied nod, took note that the warmth of the sun was beginning to seep through the fog. Then she blinked, and a sudden chill told her that something had changed.

One moment Hank was in front of her, just ten yards or so ahead, and the next moment he was gone.

Grace instantly came to a halt, and it was a good thing she did because she nearly stumbled right over the path marker, telling her that she had reached the south side.

She glanced around and turned in a circle, and still, there was no sight, no sound, no evidence of Hank, or anyone else for that matter.

Creepy, she thought, as a soft, snorted giggle escaped. But before heading back to the bridge and from there to the church, she bent over the path marker and recited its message:

You've come upon the path of Archangel Michael,
Ruling angel of the south.
Courage to face the truth is his specialty,
With support, guidance, and love.
Follow the steps set out for you,
And your purpose under God shall be revealed.

CHAPTER 13

It didn't take long for Grace to realize the flaw in her plan.

She didn't consider herself particularly religious, yet she habitually attended Sunday Mass week after week and year after year no matter where she might be. In fact, not attending wasn't something she considered an alternative.

So, just before closing the day before and while unpacking a new delivery, Grace nonchalantly raised the subject of religious preferences in hopes of getting a feel for what she would be in for. She discovered that Charlie was Presbyterian and Allie Catholic.

Forearmed with that information, and seeing as there was only one place of worship for each religious preference here in St. Thad, Grace not only chose to attend the later morning Mass—hoping that would lessen her chances of running into Allie or anyone else she knew—but she also made sure to arrive several minutes late, assuming her presence at the rear of the nave would go unnoticed as she quietly slipped inside.

But the flaw in that plan became evident the moment Grace spotted Ainsley and Alec standing in a pew several rows ahead, scanning the crowd of parishioners behind them.

Grace sunk deep into her seat—as deep as one could into a hard wooden bench—her efforts wasted as the twins spotted her even before she got settled. The two bounced with exuberance and called out, inciting a bevy of laughter, as well as a few scowls and admonishments. Their uncle, who sat between them, urged the pair back into their seats, but not without searching Grace out for himself.

From over Colin's shoulder, their gazes met his initial expression one of surprise, followed by a knowing grin and familiar nod.

A rush of heat skittered up Grace's arms, climbed her neck, and singed her ears, whether from embarrassment or guilty pleasure, she wasn't sure.

The former was nothing new—Grace could handle embarrassing moments like a pro. As for the latter, past experience was evidence enough that she didn't have the first clue as to how to handle a man's attentions. And this one did something to her insides she'd never experienced before.

Was it the way those dark eyes always seemed to be searching her own that caused the flutters? she asked herself. Or the adorable way his hair curled over the back of his neck and the tips of his ears? Or maybe it was that mischievous, I'm-up-to-no-good crooked grin.

When next the congregation stood, Ainsley looked back and waved with the enthusiasm only a child could possess. Grace offered a smile but no more before indicating to the girl that she should give her attention to the altar.

Kneeling, Grace clasped her hands together and closed her eyes. *I never should have agreed to escort those kids to the hardware store. What was I thinking? And how am I supposed to pull back from them now, I ask you?*

Half an hour later, and intent on making her escape the moment Mass ended, Grace joined the others who had already filled the aisles, only to be foiled as Allie apprehended her from behind.

She introduced Grace to her husband, her son Connor, and mother-in-law before leaning close and whispering, "I'm pretty shocked to see you here, Grace."

"I never said I was an atheist, Allie."

"No, but just yesterday, you specifically asked me whether or not I attended church services and never once mentioned that you planned

67

to. If you had, I would have saved you a seat. And to be honest, Grace, you don't give people the impression you're particularly religious."

"That's because I'm not. Particularly," Grace replied with a nonchalant lift of one shoulder.

Allie laughed as if the comment had been made in jest.

As they reached the vestibule where the priest stood, greeting his parishioners, Grace put her head down and stepped to the outside.

One more failed plan on her part because Father Stephen, apparently, didn't miss a thing.

"Ah, our newest St. Thaddean," he said, encompassing both of her hands in his and giving them a squeeze. "Welcome, Grace, welcome. It's so good to see you again. Have you got something for me today?"

"Um..." Grace flicked a furtive glance at Allie, who stood less than a foot away, observing the exchange with interest. "I do, actually."

Pulling an envelope from the pocket of her coat, Grace slipped it into the priest's grasp. "Thank you, Father."

"Of course." After a few more shared words, Grace shuffled along with the crowd, increasing her speed the second she reached the steps outside. Only to be waylaid again and this time by Duncan Haney.

"Yo, Grace!"

Coming to a halt, Grace turned and shoved both hands in her coat pockets. "Duncan. Nice to see you."

"You too," he said, sounding a little out of breath. "Listen, I don't mean to hold you up, but Florence asked me to check on things. You still having trouble with that kitchen sink?"

The drain cleaner Grace purchased from the hardware store hadn't made an iota's worth of difference. The sink was just as clogged as it was before, and the stench emanating from that side of the house was so off-putting she had yet to work up an appetite the last four days running.

Knowing the hardware store was closed on Sundays, just as the bookstore and many other businesses in town, she didn't hesitate to admit defeat. "Yes, I'm afraid so. If I drop a key off to you in the morning, do you think you could go by tomorrow while I'm at the bookstore and see what you can do?"

"Oh, I don't know, Grace." Duncan shook his head and pursed his lips. "Could be detrimental to your health, putting it off any longer. How about later today?"

"Today? I don't—" From the corner of her eye, Grace saw Colin shaking hands with Father Stephen, and right behind him stood Mrs. Haney and the twins. "Okay. Sure. I'll see you at the house in just a bit."

She got no more than three steps away before Duncan stopped her. "Uh, Grace, we've got some plans for this afternoon that Lizbeth won't want me getting out of. How's seven this evening sound?"

Throwing one last glance behind her, Grace saw the twins reaching the bottom step and knew she had to make a decision, and fast, so she took the only one she felt brave enough to endure.

CHAPTER 14

Less than two minutes later, Grace felt the weight of a long afternoon in anticipation of Duncan's arrival pressing on her shoulders. Fearing another lapse in her resolve—it hadn't been a particularly good week in that regard—she decided it would be best to stay within plain view of the public for as long as possible before returning home. So, as a number of St. Thad residents had chosen the park on this bright and sunny day, she did as well. Only, instead of heading home, Grace turned toward town square.

There, she browsed the store windows for as long as she could without looking like some lost soul, then stopped in at Pat's Hoagies for a bite to eat.

No one could avoid having a conversation with Pat; his booming voice and cheery demeanor wouldn't permit it. And surprising enough to Grace, she found she didn't mind. Pat never asked questions, and more often than not, did all the talking, which suited her just fine. The man didn't gossip either. He told her where to find the nearest hiking trails, the closest waterfall, the best fishing spot, and other hidden jewels he insisted she shouldn't miss.

Each time she stopped in for lunch, Pat would recite for her another piece of history of the Town of St. Thaddaeus. Today, as she savored a sausage and cheese calzone, he told her more about Angel Tree Farms and how that one business alone had allowed the town to thrive for over a hundred years going.

Eventually, Grace headed for home, but again, she took the long way. In no hurry to be alone with her past, especially while in her current frame of mind, she meandered through the park and even took some time to enjoy the scenery from the height of the arched bridge for several long contemplative minutes.

When she turned to leave, she saw Hank leaning against a railing, flanked by a group of teenagers deep in conversation. He nodded, acknowledging her presence, and she nodded in return, but in no mood for another smarmy conversation, Grace moved on, returning to the economy-sized house on the far side of town, much earlier than planned.

It was nearing three o'clock when she unlocked the front door and stepped inside, only to be smacked in the face with the smell of dirty-dishwater coming from the kitchen.

Fed up, she stomped toward the back door, threw it open, and let in some fresh air before returning to the living room where she lit a candle hoping to mask the stench. Blowing out a heavy sigh, she began to pace the tiny living space.

"Duncan Haney is a perfectly nice man," she mumbled, reminding herself yet again there was no reason whatsoever to be anxious. Then a thought hit, and she froze as if glued to the floor.

What if Zee comes with him?

"No problem. You'll just take a walk is all. A long one."

She circled the room a few more times, even tried watching TV, then reading, but still couldn't settle. Eventually, she curled up into a corner of the sofa, pulled a throw over her, and was shivering beneath it when it finally dawned on her that all this time she had left the back door open wide. With a shake of her head, Grace jumped to her feet and rushed into the kitchen.

As she entered, an overwhelming sensation that another presence did as well followed her. She turned full circle, searching every corner of the room but saw nothing out of sorts. Just off the kitchen was the mudroom, which doubled as a laundry room—a space she

71

estimated could be no more than a six by six square with no windows and only the one entrance. She peeked into the room and again saw no bogeyman waiting to grab her.

Without having to move an inch from where she stood, Grace next reached for the knob on the rear door, and while pulling it closed, she stuck her head out and took a quick scan of the backyard, finding it empty, and the only footprints in the snow were less than two inches in diameter.

After securely locking the door, and more out of frustration than fear, she halfheartedly searched the remainder of the house before starting a fire in the hearth.

Somewhat settled, and with two hours still to go, she showered and changed into comfy pants and a favored old sweater to wait for the handyman's arrival. And in an effort to keep her mind occupied until then, Grace next sat in the center of a double bed with a lap desk perched atop her folded legs composing another letter.

...I've tried to believe. I wanted so badly to have faith as you instructed time and again, but it was so hard to grasp, so impossible to hold that faith in my heart when each time they took me from you, the realities of life would return.

Still, I stand by the promise I made, and even though it may seem like I've given up, I haven't. Not really. Each day I continue to push through, and when the doubts return, I repeat your words until this ache in my heart eventually settles.

My relapse the other day aside, I'm doing okay here in St. Thaddaeus. As small towns go, this one is just as the tales proclaim. The people here have no qualms about getting into your personal business, and yes, there's something about this place that appears to be not quite real upon first glance, but it takes only a second look to see it's a place filled with characters of all sorts, and where gossip and speculation are a competitive sport.

I see their sidelong glances, spy them whispering behind their hands, and see the questions in their eyes. But for the most part, if someone has a real concern, they simply come right out and give it a voice.

To my astonishment, and I'm sure yours as well, I find that I appreciate the straightforward approach. In fact, Allie (the co-worker I told you about) informed me of a rumor going around town that I'm hiding from the law. I'll admit that news had my heart stuttering for a minute, and of course, I laughed when she repeated the tale.

But when she next came right out and asked if Grace St. John is my real name, I was so stunned that I nearly dropped the stack of books I was carrying. Even worse, I wasn't sure how to respond, which means I hesitated, and that was a tell in itself, wasn't it?

Among all the morals, manners, and rules you so patiently drummed into me, telling the truth is one I've always strived to obey. And hadn't you told me too, that to withhold the whole truth is the same as telling a lie?

Well, in any case, nothing should come of it because what should it matter who I am or what I call myself?

Still, I can't help but feel exposed as if a piece of the armor I keep securely in place has been loosened and pulled from its pins.

Still missing you,
Grace

CHAPTER 15

In the year 1868, a group of twenty-four settlers with huge plans, purchased two thousand acres each in a remote mountainous area of Colorado, raw land they believed to contain rich and fertile soil.

The story, as Colin learned in school, went that Thaddaeus Gall, one of those original twenty-four, contributed from his personal coffers the sums needed to begin the planting of what would later be named Angel Tree Farms. The first trees planted—a variety of maple—started it all, and thus became the name of the road where the first homes stood.

Only eleven of those original lodgings remain today as some had succumbed to fire, others to time. The house where Grace now resided, a single-story, two-bedroom bungalow, had fared better than most, although as Colin stepped up onto the tiny front porch, he couldn't help but take note of the spots where paint had begun to peel, and a growing number of boards showed evidence of rot.

He didn't remember it looking this sad the last time he'd been here.

Juggling his toolbox in one hand and takeout in the other, Colin knocked on the Maple Street door and waited. From the corner of his eye, he caught a twitch of a curtain behind the window to his left. Another thirty seconds passed until finally, a measly three-inch crack in the door appeared.

Grace's gaze flew from Colin to his pick-up parked at the curb and back again. "Where's Duncan?"

"Pop asked me to cover for him."

"Oh, but... Um..." Although she hesitated, Grace allowed a few more inches of opening between the door jamb and her foot. "Are the twins with you?"

Colin bit back a grin. "Too much ice cream, I'm afraid. They're already down for the count."

"So, you came alone then?"

Doing his best not to let the look of panic on her face worm its way into his conscience, Colin tried to keep things light. "Alec's pretty good with a hammer, but plumbing's not really his thing, and Ainsley tends to get a little bossy, she likes to take the lead. I thought maybe I could handle this one on my own." The smile he got out of Grace might have been shaky, but it was there.

"I'm sorry," she replied with an emphatic shake of her head. "I think it would be best if you came back tomorrow."

"But I brought dinner." Colin lifted the bag of takeout.

"Dinner?"

"Well, with your sink backed up, I figured you probably weren't cooking, so..." Grace only stared. "It's from Pat's," he went on. "I wasn't sure what you like, so I got some lasagna, an order of chicken cacciatore, two house salads, and a side of meatballs."

"Meatballs?"

"Yeah, I thought the meatballs would be a safe bet."

He jiggled the toolbox in his other hand, making its contents rattle. "Are you going to let me come in? It's kinda cold out here."

Almost as if on cue, Grace shivered and hugged her elbows. She glanced behind her into the house, then back out to the street, all the while nibbling on that sexy bottom lip and making him crazed. She sent furtive glances in the direction of neighboring homes where soft light glowed in the windows, and all the while, Colin kept his gaze focused only on her.

Finally, she sighed, stepped back, and waved him inside.

Colin studied the small space, wondering what Grace might have added or taken away since the last time he'd been here. He hoped to spot something, just one personal item that would give a hint as to who Grace St. John really was. But other than noting that the place had been thoroughly cleaned and dusted—he knew this because his brother's favored model of a '57 Chevy pick-up gleamed from its place on a nearby bookshelf—he saw nothing but mismatched, worn-out furniture and otherwise empty yellowed walls.

The small fire in the brick hearth grabbed several of his senses." Do I smell...chocolate cake?"

Grace's mouth quirked as she motioned toward a candle in a glass jar sitting on the mantle. "If that's all you smell, it's well worth the ten bucks it cost me."

Colin chuckled and set his toolbox down near the entrance to the kitchen. "What do you say we eat while the food's still relatively hot and tackle the sink afterward?"

"I suppose..." As she looked around, appearing unsure what to do with him, Colin took a moment to let his gaze wander as well. Starting at the bottom, he saw that she wore thick pink socks on her feet, no shoes, and what he thought women called yoga pants. She'd pushed the sleeves of her oversized gray sweater up to her elbows, bringing his gaze to the soft skin of her forearm and from there up to her shoulder and those honey-blonde curls.

His gaze snapped back to her arm where a wide bandage covered the inside of her wrist, then moved up from there, stopping to linger on the creamy but slightly puckered skin just above it. There were nearly half a dozen tiny scars that he could see from where he stood a few feet away, all thin, slightly paler than the rest of her skin, and slightly raised, most no more than two inches in length. His gaze then shot to her other arm, but just as it did, Grace shoved at her sleeves and turned toward the fireplace.

He had a moment's thought that maybe this had been a lousy idea. Maybe he'd read her wrong, and the attraction was all one-sided. Or maybe his father's attempt at matchmaking was simply more a shove than a push and one that Grace was in no way ready for or receptive to.

Hell, maybe *he* was in no way ready for *her*.

Then again, from what he'd heard, her plans were to stay only through the holidays, and if he wanted any chance at all to find out one way or the other, that didn't leave him many more chances to finagle opportunities like the one he had now.

Standing straight and tall now as if determined to put on a good front, Grace waved him toward the hearth and a gold and brown plaid sofa, its arms worn and the material frayed.

"You're right," she said. "If we're going to eat, we should do that first. Once you get past the smell of chocolate cake, you'll lose your appetite, and I wouldn't want your good deed to go unappreciated."

With poise and an air of caution, Grace lowered herself to perch on the edge of the sofa, practically hugging its corner. Taking a seat on the opposite end—the sofa was the only seating in the small room—Colin sank into the cushion a little more than expected, then struggled to lean far enough forward to lay everything out on the coffee table.

He cleared his throat. "I think I remembered to grab everything we'll need. I've got utensils, napkins, extra tomato sauce..." With the bag now empty, Colin frowned, then a moment later recalled where he'd put their drinks.

He stood to retrieve his toolbox, and from the corner of his eye, he saw Grace flinch at his sudden movement. Pretending not to notice, he pulled out two carbonated beverages, one light, one dark, and when he returned to his seat, he took care to keep his steps slow and easy.

As he presented Grace with her choices, Colin noticed it was caution that held a prominent place in those green and silver-flecked eyes, not fear as he'd previously thought. She hesitated before accepting his offer, but she did, and to his delight appeared to relax a bit more.

Colin filled their plates with a sampling of everything as Grace spread a napkin over her knees. "Salad?"

She nodded, taking the closed container he offered and flicking a glance in his direction from under her lashes. "Thank you for this. I don't know if it's the smell of fresh-baked garlic bread or the sight of Pat's lasagna, but all of a sudden, I'm famished."

"I'm pretty hungry myself. The twins insisted on mac and cheese for dinner—third time this week. Not one of my personal favorites."

"Can I ask...?" Instead of completing her question, Grace shook her head and took a bite of lasagna.

"You're wondering where their mother and father are?"

"It's none of my business."

And a subject I really don't like discussing. But...

Colin sipped from his can of soda then sat back with his plate in his lap. "I've never met their mother, and from all I know about her, I'm glad. Angela, that's her name, had no idea she was carrying twins until the day they were born, and that alone tells me more than I care to know. Although I suppose I should give her *some* credit. According to my brother, Angela did manage to keep off the 'really *hard* drugs' during her pregnancy. He may have been telling the truth, too, because Alec and Ainsley are as healthy and normal as can be."

Grace huffed out a breath. "I'm sorry, but there's no excuse for such negligence." She paused, then asked, "Does that mean she reverted to using again after they were born?"

Colin chewed and swallowed. "From what I understand, it got worse. Apparently, she never wanted one baby, let alone two, and couldn't handle the responsibility."

"Not couldn't. Didn't care to."

"My thoughts exactly," he said, taking note of Grace's hardened expression and the firm set of her jaw.

A long minute passed in silence before she spoke again. "How is it you never met their mother? Have you been out of the country or something?"

"I've lived here all my life, with the exception of the two years I went away for college. That was right about the time the twins were born." Grace gave him a puzzled look. "No, I didn't go right out of high school," Colin explained. "I waited because we agreed I would. We couldn't afford for both my brother and me to go at the same time."

"Where did you go to school?"

"Colorado State University."

"That's in Fort Collins, isn't it? North of Denver."

With his mouth full, Colin nodded. "It's an agricultural school and seemed like the best choice if I wanted to take over management of Angel Tree Farms someday. That had been my plan at the time."

"Had been?"

Colin shrugged. "Plans change—dreams with them. The twins are what's important now—their sense of security and stability. Making sure they have all the love and nurturing a child needs and deserves."

Grace froze, a fork only inches from her lips, her face unreadable. She looked directly into Colin's eyes for the first time since he'd arrived and seemed to be searching for evidence of something important.

After a long moment, she asked, "You really mean that, don't you?"

"Of course. I mean everything I say. Unless I'm teasing," he added with a wink.

Without taking that bite, she dropped the fork onto her plate and sat back with a sigh. Colin watched as a myriad of emotions crossed over her face, all of them too brief to decipher.

He got the feeling a good reason for her uncertainty of him—her uncertainty of everyone here from what he'd heard—lurked somewhere not far beyond those invisible walls of hers. So he waited, and after a time, Grace seemed to make up her mind about something; perhaps, it was to trust him, if even only a little.

She looked down at her half-eaten meal. "I didn't mean to question your sincerity. I don't know why I always—"

"I'm sure you've got your reasons."

"That's no excuse for being rude."

"You weren't rude, Grace. You don't know me, and how could you, unless you ask questions?"

"Still..."

"Still," he repeated with amusement in his tone, "I don't mind you questioning my integrity as long as you admit your mistake. I'm a damn nice guy," he added with a wiggle of his brows," and you couldn't trust anyone more than me with your secrets." Her reaction to that comment wasn't the smile he'd aimed for and told Colin his teasing had put her on guard again.

"Anyway," he continued, "getting back to your initial question, I was in Fort Collins, and my brother Camdyn was still in California. See, we had another agreement, Cam and I, one just between us. He would get his degree first, then come back home and help Pop with the store while I went to school."

"But your brother reneged on the deal?"

"Yeah. And not one of us saw it coming. Me, Pop, Mom. We had no idea he'd dropped out of school early, or that he'd gotten some drug addict pregnant."

The anger and hurt Colin hadn't yet learned to control must have shown in either his face or his voice. It was the only reason he could think of to explain why Grace reached out and covered his hand with her own. And why she looked just as surprised by the comforting gesture as he was.

He instantly turned his palm up to encompass hers and took hold. It was the first time they had touched and felt more right than Colin could have dreamed possible. But the intimacy of the moment ended almost as quickly as it began. Grace pulled away and tucked her now clasped hands between her knees.

"So, uh...how did the twins end up here. With you?"

Mentally shrugging his disappointment aside, Colin answered, "Angela threatened to leave unless Cam did something to 'relieve her stress.' So he brought her and the twins here with the idea that having an accessible support system would solve their problems."

"So, you came home to help."

"Not at first. Mom cut back her hours at the library and took over care of the twins for as much as she could manage while my brother worked part-time for Pop and part-time at Angel Tree Farms. I got the lowdown on what was going on but was ordered by my parents to stay in school and finish my degree. They assured me everything here was fine, but I'd planned to see for myself, anyway, as soon as the semester ended. I would have come home sooner, but I was juggling as many classes as I could handle to finish quicker, as well as working evenings and weekends to cover living expenses.

"In the meantime," Colin went on, "while everyone else is busting their butts, Angela's living a life of leisure. No job to go to, no kids to worry about for hours at a time, free room and board... Only big brother miscalculated on something else, according to Pop. See, getting a hold of illegal drugs in this town might be far from simple, but it's not impossible."

"Their mother should have been in rehab."

"That's what I said." Colin swallowed the guilt that ate at him daily for not having been around to help.

"Anyway, next I hear, things aren't going so well. Mom finds the twins home alone one day, thank God they were safe in their crib, while their mother's out doing God knows what with who the hell knows. Then Pop stops by to check on things the next day and walks in on Angela throwing a temper tantrum over something or another. Alec's crying his little heart out, and Ainsley's cowering under that kitchen table in there with her thumb in her mouth and her eyes as big as walnuts."

"Wait," Grace interrupted. "That kitchen table in there?" she asked, pointing in the direction he'd indicated.

"Yeah, Cam and his family were living here at the time."

"Well, that explains a few things," Grace said with a nod and a wave for him to continue.

Colin wasn't sure what it explained, but he went on anyway. "So, my parents made some ultimatums and gave Cam the night to decide what he was going to do. What choice Cam made, I'm not completely sure, but that's when Mommy Dearest decided she was done playing house because that same night, Angela broke into the St. Thad Medical Clinic and stole a bunch of prescription meds. To make matters worse, a nurse who was on duty at the time got in the way."

In response to Grace's gasp, he added, "Mrs. Tillman, the nurse, she's okay. Now. She got her head cracked open but no lasting damage, thank God."

"Oh, Colin, I'm so sorry. So, their mother's in jail, then?"

"It wouldn't surprise me, but honestly, I have no idea. By the time Chief Daniels put together the evidence he needed to make an arrest, Angela had skipped town."

Grace pushed her plate away, the look on her face saying she couldn't stomach another bite. She sucked in a breath and let it out with a slow exhale. "Which explains why Alec said his mother was lost."

"Probably not the best explanation Mom and Pop could have given them, but how do you explain something like that to a toddler? Of course, I'm just as much to blame. I haven't come up with anything better since, and they're probably old enough now to understand a bit more. Instead, I've chosen to avoid the conversation altogether."

Grace nodded as if she understood. "And their father? Where's he?"

"Good question." Scraping up the dregs from his plate and shoving what little was left in his mouth, Colin chewed and swallowed before going on. "Cam lasted not quite six months on his own, and when I think back to the last conversations we had, I can honestly say I'm pretty sure he hated every minute of it. See, Cam despised working at the tree farm, that wasn't his thing, and I don't think he gave a damn about the hardware store either. Plus... Well, the rest is just a suspicion, so I'll keep that to myself.

"Anyway, I'd come home for the summer—hadn't been back more than a few weeks—and big brother drops Ainsley and Alec off with Mom, same as always, but this time he leaves a note in their diaper bag saying he's going to find Angela and bring her back. By the time Mom discovers the note, Cam's long gone and not answering his cell phone."

"So..." Watching Grace as she appeared to struggle with her words, Colin saw anguish, heartbreak, and disgust move over her features. "Their mother's not going to come back, is she? Not voluntarily, and not when she knows she'll be arrested the minute she steps back in this town?"

"I can't see that she would."

"What do you expect will happen when your brother finds her?"

Colin let out a mirthless laugh. "Grace. We're long past wondering about Angela. That was a little over two years ago."

"Two years?" Grace stood, her movements disconnected and jerky as she stepped toward the fire as if to warm herself. The look on her face from what Colin could make out as she stared into the flames, had a fierceness to it. That, and some kind of acceptance. He could imagine the thoughts going through her head.

Then her expression changed again. "Wait a minute," Grace said, looking even more stricken than before. "Does that mean your brother's been gone—"

"About eighteen months now."

CHAPTER 16

"He left his children? Left them while he's out there searching for someone who probably doesn't even want to be found?" Grace practically spit the words from between clenched teeth. *She's good and angry now*, Colin thought, as she nearly vibrated with it.

Just as he started to speak, she began firing off questions like, "When did you last hear from him?" and "Doesn't he realize these children need him more?" But before he could answer a single one, she went on with, "Alec and Ainsley seem so happy and well-adjusted. I never suspected—"

"You know," Colin interrupted with a raise of his brows, "I get that you'd see things from the twins' point of view, it makes sense with your history, although it doesn't say much for what you think of me or my parents."

A flush of heat crept up Grace's neck, and over her cheekbones, then anger took over as his words undoubtedly sank in. She turned her back to him, out of embarrassment, he presumed. "I see Allie wasted no time."

"Allie was only dispelling the rumors of your supposed Bonnie and Clyde existence. Don't be mad at her."

Grace shrugged and looked down at her feet. "I can't be mad about the truth. But I don't deserve anyone's pity either. So I was abandoned as an infant and given a name by the man who found me. So what. That doesn't mean I know how the twins feel. I never knew my parents, never had a family."

She sighed. "That aside, I owe you an apology for what I said about the twins being well-adjusted. That didn't come out right, and I didn't mean to imply—"

"Jeez, Grace, don't beat yourself up. I was only teasing."

"I'm getting the impression that's a favorite pastime of yours," she mumbled while huffing out an impatient breath. "Why is it I can't seem to ever say the right thing around you?"

"I'll take that to mean my presence has an effect on you, same as yours does on me."

Colin stood then too, his intention to cut the distance between them.

"Don't. Please," she said with a stiff arm jutting out in front of her. Taking a step back, she came into contact with the hearth.

"You don't need to be afraid of me."

Grace snorted a laugh that held no humor. "Maybe you're the one who needs to be cautious. Look," she began rushing her next words, "I'm probably being presumptuous, but I should tell you that I don't date. Plus, I'm only here for a few more weeks, in any case, so—"

"So, what's wrong with enjoying each other's company while we can? And what do you mean you don't date?"

She wrapped her arms around her elbows and hugged herself as he eased his way close enough to touch. "Let's just say I lug around a lot of baggage. More than anyone cares to handle or should have to. Besides, it's not just that I don't date; I don't do relationships of any kind, friend or otherwise. But I made a promise to help Charlie get through the holidays, and I'd like to follow through with that if I can. I just need to be left alone."

"Then what?" Colin asked.

"Then I'll move on. That's what I do."

Colin wanted to laugh. He wanted to gather her in and convince her he could handle any baggage she cared to share. He did neither. "What about Allie, Charlie, my dad? They're your friends."

"No. Co-workers. Acquaintances. That's as far as I go."

He studied her posture, the firm set of her jaw, and decided she was as serious as Dutch Elm disease. But not as determined as he was.

There were visible cracks in that thick bark Grace used to protect herself, or more like hairline fractures if he was being honest; you only had to look to see them, and Colin was definitely looking.

Switching gears, he went back to the coffee table and began shoving plates and dirty napkins into the bag. "Okay, Grace. I'm not going to push, but I should warn you. Before too long, you're going to explain to me why."

"Why? Why what?"

Looking up, he gave her a hard stare and renewed his resolve. "Why you're running and from what or whom? Why you won't let anyone close enough to see the woman behind those incredible eyes of yours?" He paused. "Pop thinks you're protecting yourself from being hurt. That may be partly true, but he's wrong about the whole of it, isn't he?"

She looked him in the eyes but didn't answer. Colin shrugged, brushing away the sting of rejection and shoved one last item in the paper sack. "You can answer that one later, as well. In the meantime, I'll get started on the sink."

After retrieving his toolbox from the floor, Colin headed for the kitchen with Grace following close behind, huffing with indignation.

"You have no right to be angry," she snarled. "It's not as if I invited you here and—"

"Who says I'm angry?"

"It's written all over your face for one—" As they crossed the threshold, the stench of dirty, stagnant water slapped them both in the face. Gagging, Grace raced from the room. By the time she returned, holding a hand towel over her mouth and nose, Colin had already donned a disposable respirator mask and was positioning himself under the sink with wrench in hand.

"Grab me a bucket, would you?" he asked without glancing her way.

"Um..." Grace looked around.

"Check the broom closet in the mudroom."

"Oh. Right." Grace frowned as she exited the kitchen.

"While you're in there," Colin called out, "see if you can find more than one, I think we might need it."

As instructed, Grace went straight to a tall, skinny cabinet where she found a mop bucket sitting at the bottom. After glancing around, she saw another bucket perched on top of the cabinet, but couldn't reach it, so she turned to grab the folding step stool her landlord had left perched in a corner of the room.

As she did, her gaze locked on a bloody towel sitting on top of the dryer. A towel Grace knew for certain she had left soaking in the washing machine.

Her fingers brushed across the bandage beneath her sleeve as her thoughts raced with one possible explanation after another.

"You can't find one?" Colin's voice coming from right behind her sent Grace spinning around with a jolt. At the same time, she snatched up the towel and held it behind her back.

"Uh...um..."

He tilted his head, and Grace blinked, her thoughts still spinning wildly.

She held the mop bucket out to him. "I was just getting the step stool so I could grab that second bucket for you," she explained, pointing to the one perched on the top of the cabinet.

"Oh. I'll get it." Of course, seeing as he was about half a foot taller than she was, Colin had no problem reaching it without the aid.

While his back was turned, Grace slipped the bloody hand towel into the washing machine and followed him out.

Once back in the kitchen, Colin strategically placed the mop bucket under the sink and went back to work.

"How did you know about the closet in the mudroom?" she asked.

Colin's gaze flicked briefly in her direction. "Don't go imagining anything nefarious, Grace. I've been in this house a few dozen times over the years. That's all."

She had no doubt that was true, but the idea that Colin was so familiar with this house didn't make her any less wary.

He pulled the pipe apart, allowing the bucket to fill with dirty water, then held out a hand for the second. After he switched them around, Grace carried the one now filled to the brim outside the back door, again, making sure it was securely locked when she returned.

By that time, Colin was already on his feet. "Well, here's your problem," he said with a snort of laughter as he pulled the soggy carcass of an engorged rat from the pipe and held it out to her.

Grace let out a scream and took a huge step backward. Unable to stop her momentum, she tripped over a kitchen chair and went down hard, bumping against a rickety china cabinet that began to rock.

Next thing she knew, approximately one hundred eighty pounds of male surrounded her on all sides as she was simultaneously rolled across the kitchen, coming to a full stop with a jolt and an "*oomph*" from Colin as they butted up against the refrigerator.

A split second later, the china cabinet tilted just enough to send the overflow of items perched on top crashing to the floor.

Lightning bright dots burst behind Grace's eyelids as her breath seized, and her entire body began to shake.

Colin tightened his hold and ducked his head covering her completely as something shattered, and next came the bounce and clang of a heavy pot, followed by books, papers and who knows what else slapping against the yellowing vinyl.

A long moment passed in silence while Grace laid there with her eyes squeezed shut, her limbs tensed, trying desperately not to freak out.

Colin pulled back and lifted his head. "Are you all right?" he asked, sliding his hands down her arms.

Every muscle in Grace's body shook so badly that had she not had her jaw locked in place, she was sure her teeth would chatter. She was headed straight into a panic attack and knew she had to pull herself out of it, and quickly.

"Get off me," she managed between clenched teeth. Her bottom lip quivered as Colin stared at her with an expression of confusion. "Get off, get off, get off!"

He moved quickly, and after setting her free, Grace sat up, curled into a ball, and fisted her hands. The only sounds she heard now were her own ragged breathing, and Colin moving around the kitchen.

Judging by the cursing she heard coming from under his breath, she assumed he was cleaning up the mess he'd caused but knew better when a warm cloth touched her forehead. She took it and nodded a thanks as he moved away, then the scraping of a chair followed.

Once she had herself under some semblance of control, Grace looked up to find him sitting in a kitchen chair a foot away with his elbows on his knees. His eyes were full of apology, and just as Grace began to speak, he interrupted her as usual.

"Mom has knocked me upside the head enough times that I should know better, and still, every once in a while, I let my teasing get out of control." He paused. "I'm so, so incredibly sorry, Grace."

"Don't be." Her voice came out barely more than a whisper. "I'm the one who's sorry; I should never have let it go this far. I'd just hoped..."

"Hoped what, Grace?"

She swallowed back a sob and tried again. "I'd just hoped." She sighed. "And that's where I went wrong. I should never have allowed it to go this far."

After a brief hesitation, his eyes searching hers, he asked, "Why did you, do you think?"

She studied his gaze, and the concerned expression marring those handsome features. His hair was tousled, which made him all the more endearing. She yearned to touch—wanted so badly to feel his arms around her again, only this time gently. Caressingly, Lovingly.

"Be honest," he added.

Grace shrugged and dried her nearly overflowing eyes with what she now realized was a kitchen towel before sucking in a deep, fortifying breath. "Partly because of another promise I'd made a long time ago. And partly because there's something about this town...about you that makes me want to."

Another long silence stretched between them before Colin nodded and stood. "All right, Grace. This is what we're going to do. You're going to take a hot bath or lie down or whatever while I clean up the mess I caused. Then I'll leave and lock the door behind me. Okay?"

She forced herself to take the hand he offered to help her to her feet. As she rose to her full height, he gently cupped her cheeks, ignored her flinch and the fist that instinctively formed, and laid a soft kiss on her brow. Then, before she could recoil or say anything more, he turned away and bent to pick something up from beneath the table.

Grace stood there without moving, unsure what to say or even what to do. Should she explain, apologize, ask him to stay? Or accept that she'd failed again before even trying?

She looked up, took a breath, and opened her mouth to speak, then paused as she caught sight of Colin's stricken expression as he stared down at the clear plastic bag he now held in his hands.

"What's that?"

Colin pressed his lips into a straight line and swore under his breath. "Well, if this isn't yours, then I'm guessing it's evidence."

CHAPTER 17

A sliver of moonlight shone in between the window blinds providing just enough light for someone to cross the floor unimpeded, although not enough to make out the shadows that lurked in the night.

It took Grace forever to fall asleep in the quiet room, but she knew she had when something, some sound, pulled her awake.

Her eyes flew open, and her breath seized. She lay motionless, listening, allowing only her gaze to shift, but not a muscle more.

No sounds came, and nothing moved, but *something* had awakened her, and the sensation of another presence looming near was palpable.

She flattened her hands against the cool sheet and began sliding them under her pillow. A split second later, a slight dip in the mattress caused her to stiffen and freeze, and just as quickly came the ragged breath at her ear and a hand over her mouth.

She squeezed her eyes closed, but only for a moment, while swallowing a whimper as those fingers slid over her spine from top to bottom, their slow, patient stroke both possessive and intent.

Sweat broke out of every pore as she bit into her bottom lip and began reciting a litany of pleas.

Not again. Not here. Please, please, no more.

His body followed, pinning her to the sheets, then came a hushed laugh, both wicked and familiar, striking her inner ear like hot bursts of venom.

His moist tongue burned her lobe and scorched her neck as it slid along her skin, and his stifling weight bared down on her lower body.

The hand covering her mouth disappeared just long enough to wrap long fingers around her throat. A whimper escaped, and while his other hand took hold of her breast, her own balled into fists.

Desperate for a different outcome than before, Grace struggled beneath him, and the prayers she had no faith would be heard repeated over and over in her head.

With a cutting grip, he forced her onto her back where eyes that housed no soul stared down into hers, and surrounding them a shadowed face; one remembered from old—a face she never again wanted to see and never thought she would.

A hair-raising scream erupted from between her lips as Grace pounded her fists into his shoulders and chest. She sucked in a breath, preparing to let loose with another, but a sudden punch to her belly knocked every ounce of breath from her lungs.

She woke to find herself on the floor, her breath heaving, her eyes streaming with tears.

The nightgown she wore was damp and tangled between her thighs as she rolled onto her back but didn't attempt to rise. Her insides still trembled, and her legs were too shaky to stand, so she lay there for long minutes allowing the quiet and stillness of the room to even her breathing and steady her racing heart.

It was only a dream, she told herself, again and again, a memory that refused to fade and be lost.

Swiping her cheeks with the backs of her hands, Grace rose and with clumsy steps, made her way down the darkened hallway.

Her skin itched from dried sweat, and her clothes stuck to her skin. Staring into the bathroom mirror, she saw her face was blotchy, her eyes swollen and red, so she stripped and turned the hot water on full blast.

Now showered, and dry she went in search of clean sheets for the sweat-soaked bed, and there in the tiny linen closet, she found what she needed; a stack in soft blue sat on a top shelf.

Stretching onto her tiptoes, she reached up and yanked at an edge, and with a few more tugs, the whole stack came tumbling down, landing right in her arms. But a lump between the folds had her dumping her find on the floor.

Her movements were slow and hesitant as she eased down onto her knees, then pulled the top sheet away to reveal what looked like a child's pencil box hidden beneath.

With extreme caution, she opened the lid and peeked inside, then sat back on her heels and let out a sigh.

CHAPTER 18

After staring at a blank ceiling for the past three nights, any patience Colin might have possessed had been worn thin by the time he handed the twins off to their preschool teacher.

He attributed a good part of that loss of sleep to Grace. Something had happened to her in the past, and he didn't like any one of the dozen or so possibilities that wouldn't leave his head. He wanted to sooth and make promises he couldn't keep-not if she wouldn't even let him in. He also wanted to know what was behind those eyes: the pain, the passion, the hopes, and the dreams.

Closing his own eyes, Colin saw the whole scene in her kitchen again. He could feel the way she shook beneath him, see the pain and despair in her eyes, and hear the tremble in her voice when she said, *"I'd just hoped."*

He wanted to know what she meant by that, but he was no longer sure taking Grace on was a good idea. At least not right now, because during all those sleepless hours, he'd also been thinking about that blasted plastic bag filled with an assortment of pills, and what its presence there meant.

So, after dropping the kids off at preschool, Colin decided it was time to find out. He took a detour and headed straight to the police station, figuring that with any luck, he could get in and out before Pop started to wonder why he was late getting to the hardware store.

Unfortunately, he must have left whatever luck he might have had coming at home because his early arrival at the station house had him cooling his heels in the Chief's office, waiting for Daniels to appear.

Added to that, when the police chief did finally mosey in half an hour later, he obliged Colin to wait some more while he handed something over to his deputy, fixed himself a mug of coffee and joked with his dispatcher about some kids rearranging the Catholic church's nativity scene in a lewd manner.

After overhearing most of the story, and satisfied that he now knew what had kept the police chief this morning, Colin tried not to laugh.

His amusement was quickly lost, however, when Daniels followed that delay by taking several more minutes to hunt up the two-year-old police report, and then get himself situated behind his desk.

As former coach, P.E. teacher, and student counselor at St. Thaddeaus School, Daniels was well-known, well-loved, and well-respected. He'd earned that love and respect by drumming into his students a strict code of conduct, manners, morals, and self-discipline. Although Colin's school days were far behind him, he still respected Daniels but was no longer intimidated by him. So when the police chief looked him in the eyes and sat there with his arms folded over his chest, waiting for his former student to start talking, Colin did so without feeling the need to squirm.

Colin relayed the entire Sunday evening story. Well, not the *entire* story as the majority of that evening would stay between him and Grace, but he did tell the chief about how he'd gone to the Old Cambroto place to fix the kitchen sink, and how he'd been teasing and inadvertently scared Grace enough that she tripped and bumped into the china cabinet causing it to sway just enough for the butt-load of items on top to come tumbling down, in particular, the plastic bag he now pulled from the toolbox at his feet and slapped down on the desk.

During the telling, Daniels had narrowed his eyes and grunted a few times, but said little else.

As Colin's story reached its end, the chief sucked in air through his nose and sat back, his arms still crossed over his chest. "You could have just flushed this stuff down the toilet. Why bring it to me?"

"I considered that, but Mom and Pop need some answers, and they're not getting any with all of us burying our heads in the snow."

"Uh-huh." Daniels eyed him for a long minute, saying nothing further. Then, finally, with what looked like a great deal of reluctance, St. Thad's chief of police pulled the plastic baggie closer, opened his file, and began comparing the bag's contents to the list of stolen meds.

Long minutes passed in near silence. Colin checked his watch for the fifth time, sighed, tapped his foot, and eventually got up and started to pace. Between his loss of sleep, which amounted to a complete loss of patience, and the police chief's lack of speed—which Colin likened to watching a seed sprout—it wasn't much longer before Colin was leaning over the chief's desk, testing his skill at reading upside down.

"Unless you have a medical degree, Haney, you're not going to understand it anyway, so sit your butt down and behave yourself."

Colin obeyed, but not without letting Daniels know he wasn't happy about it. "You don't need to be able to spell it or pronounce it to see if the descriptions match what you're looking at, Chief. What the hell does it say; blue pills, pink pills, yellow capsules, what?"

Chief Daniels, a sixty-year-old man with thinning hair and a growing paunch, kept his expression stoic, allowing another long minute to pass in tense silence.

Finally, he scratched the underside of his double chin and huffed out a breath. "No way it's all of what was stolen from the clinic, but it could be some. In any case, I'd have to get this stuff tested before I can say for sure, and at this point, what's it matter?"

"It matters because if the twins' mother was the only one using, why wouldn't she have taken these with her? What's this stuff doing in the house where my brother continued to live with his kids for another six damn months after Angela split?"

Daniels raised his palms in an exaggerated shrug. "Maybe she started divvying the stuff up the minute she got home and hid some of it. You know, a little here, a little there? Then when she decided hightailing it out of town was her best bet, she either forgot where she put it all or just didn't take time to collect it."

"Yeah, right," Colin said with a snort of derision. "After going through all that trouble to get it in the first place? I'm not that gullible, and neither are you."

"Never thought you were."

"Oh, so you just hoped I'd pretend to be?" Colin stood and paced to the window and back.

"You know, Haney, it might be the best thing for your folks if you'd drop this. They've suffered plenty already with your brother taking off like he did and leaving his little ones behind."

Colin shook his head. "Mom and Pop have been asking questions about how it went that night with Grace, and they know I'm holding something back. I can't continue to keep this from them; it's not right. What I *will* do is not mention what I'm thinking unless one of them goes there on their own."

"And just what is it you're thinking?"

Colin sighed and retook his seat. "I think Camdyn was just as much part of the problem as Angela was."

"How so?"

"He wanted out. I'd known it since we were in junior high, we'd talked about it, Cam and I. And we made a deal, one just between us. He goes to school, gets his degree, then comes back and works with Pop while I go and do the same. After that, I come home to stay, and Cam goes off to wherever the hell he wants. Only, five years after Cam leaves for California, we come to find out he's supporting two babies and a drug addict off Mom and Pop's money; the money that was supposed to be paying for him to finish school."

"What are you trying to say? You think your brother planned to leave his children behind all along?"

Colin looked up, a little stunned by the chief's words, but only because it was the first time he heard them spoken from someone other than the voice in his own head. "I suspect Cam never did have any intention of returning to St. Thad. I think he hooked up with the wrong kind of people, got in over his head, and had no choice but to come back where he knew Mom and Pop would bail him out. I think Cam craves a lifestyle he believes he deserves and one that isn't conducive to this town. I think he believes he loves Angela or in some way, feels he needs to be with her, maybe because he's just as addicted to the drugs as she is, or maybe he's just addicted to *her*. Who the hell knows? Either way, Angela didn't want anything to do with being a mother, and Cam made a choice. He chose her, and he chose himself."

"He always was a selfish kid," Daniels mumbled under his breath.

Likely sensing that his former pupil had more to say, Daniels kept quiet after that and waited. Eventually, Colin said, "Every day Mom and Pop pray to God that today's the day their oldest son comes home. Today's the day he remembers he has responsibilities. But I know that isn't going to happen and my parents need to know that too. They need to be able to move past the hurt and deception."

"Sounds like you know more than you've said."

"Colin lifted one shoulder in a negligent shrug. "It's more assumption than fact. Or maybe just that I know my big brother so damn well."

"Did he ever say straight out that he wasn't coming back?"

"No," Colin replied with a snort of derision. "As you already know, Mom, Pop, and I each spoke to him on several occasions those first few months, and every time, Cam swore he was coming back, soon as he found Angela. Then he stopped answering our calls altogether, and shortly after that, the cell number we had no longer belonged to him. We lost all avenues of contact with no idea what state he was even in."

The chief nodded. "I remember. Until that last phone call."

"Right. Last February, when he called out of the blue and promised me he was on his way home."

"And nothing since?"

"Not a word."

Daniels heaved a sigh and linked his fingers over his belt buckle.

After another bout of silence, Colin asked, "So, are you going to call Doc Baxter to see if he can identify what's in that plastic bag or not?"

"We both know Doc Baxter retired last year. About now, he's likely holed up somewhere outside of Tucson."

"We also both know his son took over the practice and is running the medical clinic now. Surely Bax would have access to those records."

"Probably. Sending these off to the county lab's a better bet, though, especially if you want to keep town gossip to a minimum."

"I'll fill Pop in when I get to the store, and he can talk to Mom when he feels the time is right. As for everybody else, I'd appreciate you keeping this internal."

"What about our newest resident?"

"Grace won't say anything to anyone."

"You sound pretty sure about that."

"I am."

"Uh-huh." The chief paused. "Well, I'll do my best, but knowing the good citizens of St. Thad as I do, I won't be holding my breath. Fact is, Haney, at least one person saw you come in here this morning, and I guarantee more'll see you leave. So, if you haven't already, you might want to start composing whatever story you plan to give to anyone who asks what you were doing here."

Colin lifted the toolbox he'd left on the floor by his chair. "That faulty outlet behind you is all fixed."

Chief Daniels acknowledged the cover story with a satisfied nod.

Colin said, "The answers no, by the way. To the county lab idea. That'll take too long. I'd really appreciate having this settled sooner rather than later."

"I figured you'd nix it, damn stubborn... How about this then? I slip this supposed evidence in a drawer and forget about it for a couple of weeks? Send the stuff out for testing after the first of the year when I come across it again?"

Colin shook his head. "I need to know, and Mom and Pop are going to need some answers, too. Before Christmas, Chief. You can make it happen; I know you can."

Daniels smirked. "Flattery, Haney? I'm shocked."

Colin attempted a grin but didn't quite make it.

The chief said, "Look, I get where you're going with this. You think your brother might have had something to do with breaking into the medical clinic that night, or at the very least, you need peace of mind that he didn't. I get it. But like I told you before, Angela was the only one visible on that security tape, this isn't going to prove anything."

"Yeah, and you also said you didn't think she did it alone."

"Never said I thought your brother was her accomplice."

"Doesn't mean he wasn't. And in my mind, if the drugs in that bag are part of what was stolen, that's proof enough for me."

The police chief gave Colin a hard stare. "All right, Haney, fine. We'll do this your way. I'll stop by the clinic and see Bax soon as I can set it up."

"Thanks." Colin slapped his knees and stood.

"Hold on a sec, would you?"

With a nod, Colin once again lowered himself into the hard plastic chair.

Daniels took a long sip from his cooling coffee mug, then swiped a hand over his chin. "First, I want to preface that what I'm about to say goes no further than this room."

Colin agreed with a stiff nod, although he couldn't help but wonder where this conversation was headed.

"I imagine you heard the rumors going around about your dinner companion, Miss St. John?"

Colin blinked with both surprise and confusion. "Sure. So?"

"I want you to know that I've reprimanded my staff. All three of them," he added with a sneer. "That never should have gotten out, and I'm sorry that it did."

"Grace is the one who deserves the apology—"

"She does, and she'll be getting one, personally."

"Good."

When Colin went to stand again, the chief waved him down. "Hold on now, that's not all."

"You don't need to explain, Chief, Grace already did. It's her legal name, not an alias. Although, now that I think about it, I would like to know why you were checking up on her in the first place?"

"I wasn't checking up on her exactly, and her name has nothing to do with anything."

"Then what are you trying to tell me? That Grace really is on the run from the law?"

"Not that I'm aware of. The charges were dropped when—"

"What kind of charges?"

"Well, I can't say exactly but—"

"If you can't say why the hell did you bring it up?"

The police chief scowled and puffed out his chest. "Don't go getting belligerent, Haney. I'm trying to do you a favor here."

Colin scowled right back. "Then at least tell me this, do the charges involve drugs?"

"No, drugs have nothing to do with it."

"Child abuse?"

Daniels hesitated. "Listen to me. I only brought it up because I want to caution you about getting involved. Best advice I can give you is to leave her be. Let the woman spend the next month helping Charlie out at the bookstore. He can use it, and from what I hear, she's doing a good job. I also understand she's made it clear that she has every intention of moving on first of the year. Let her spend the up-coming holiday in peace, and you and your family do the same. You all don't need any more upheaval in your lives, especially with this new development," he finished indicating the plastic baggie still sitting on his desktop.

Colin got to his feet. He retrieved his toolbox and headed for the door, but turned back just as he crossed the threshold.

"I appreciate the warning, Chief. And I hope my saying this won't change your mind about speaking with Bax, but I have no intention of staying away from Grace. Fact is, you just made me realize I've wasted too much time already debating what my next move would be ever since I left her house on Sunday."

"Haney—"

"No, I heard you out, now you hear me. From what I can tell, Grace has been keeping her distance from everyone she comes into contact with for far too long. You only have to look into her eyes, and you can see the pain and loneliness. She isolates herself by putting up a defense shield. She's protecting herself from—"

The police chief slapped a hand down on his desktop with a loud *thwack*. It got the job done because Colin stopped his rant mid-sentence.

In a soft voice, Daniels said, "You've got it all wrong, Colin. Grace isn't protecting herself; she's protecting *you*."

CHAPTER 19

As had become Grace's habit, she walked to work, taking her chosen route through Araqiel Park. It added to her commute, as skirting the park would save time, but what fun was there in that? Besides, she reasoned with herself, today, in particular, she had plenty of time before she was due at the bookstore. Allie was opening this morning, and Grace had volunteered to take the rest of the day through closing so Allie could spend some quality time with her husband and son.

Grace stuck to the paved paths that would take her over the bridge, and with her thoughts plentiful and the park nearly empty this time of day, she couldn't help but take advantage of the solitude.

She needed to breathe, to think, to talk...

So, pulling her cell phone from her pocket, Grace called up his number and waited. On the other end, it rang and rang until—

"I'm sorry I wasn't here to take your call, but please leave a message, and I promise to get back to you as soon as I can."

Her eyes filled as she slipped the phone back into her pocket, but the tears didn't fall.

He had always been the one person she could trust to listen without judgment. The one person who knew her past, knew her secrets, knew her insecurities. But he wasn't available to be her sounding board today.

With a twist of her lips, Grace looked out at the scenery in front of her and considered.

Perhaps, she did have another option, after all. Hank was the complete opposite of the one and only person she had ever counted on. Over the past week, they had run into each other almost daily. There was something about Hank, something about his self-deprecation, maybe, that made her feel she could divulge anything, and not only would he not judge her for it, but more than likely, he would take the opposite approach by telling her he was guilty of worse.

She stepped onto the outer circle of the paved path on the northern side. Having used this route a number of times, she could already recite the words inscribed on its plaque by rote.

As you enter the path of Uriel,
Ruling angel of the north,
Forget not the knowledge
and wisdom of God's love.
Trust in the intuition Uriel offers,
Remember to allow his light to shine,
and bring with it the answers you seek.

If only she could sense that intuition or hear the angel Uriel's message in the breeze or the crunch of snow underfoot. If only she could discover the answers to questions she didn't know to ask in the chattering squeaks of the squirrels watching her from a nearby branch. But here it was only Grace's boot heals that sang in the silence.

The smell of wood smoke, decaying leaves, and the fresh scent of nature filled the air.

The town had received a few inches of fresh snow the evening before, but Mac had obviously been up early, clearing the paths as there was neither a sliver of ice nor a speck of snow on the concrete pavers.

The roar of Kutiel River drew near, a comforting rhythm that brought to mind a symphony of angels shouting to be heard over the din. Or perhaps that din *was* the angels, she mused, if indeed they existed at all.

Moving at a quickened pace, by the time Grace reached the bridge, a sheen of perspiration dotted her forehead. She unzipped her coat, pulled off her gloves, and stuck them in her pockets as she glanced around, searching for the one person who always seemed to be around.

With no sign of him and a heavy sigh of resignation, she made her way to the center of the bridge, where she stopped and leaned back to take in the view.

She hadn't seen or heard from Colin since he left her house last Sunday night, nearly a week ago now. While the disappointment of his seemingly easy retreat left a bitter taste in her mouth, Grace had to admit the fault of that was all hers.

She'd asked him to back off, to leave her alone and let her be. Just as she always did, she chose a solitary existence filled with loneliness and despair over allowing even the tiniest bit of faith and hope into her heart. And all while knowing, remembering, that she had made a promise to give faith a try.

Should she take back that promise? Should she go to Colin and beg for another chance? What would he say if she—

"Hiya, Gracie. What's cookin'?"

Grace nearly jumped out of her skin. With a hand over her thumping heart, she sent Hank what she hoped translated to a scathing glare.

"Ouch!" he said with a mocking smirk and a hand to his heart. Coming to rest directly across from her, Hank leaned against the wide wooden railing of the bridge, then proceeded to copy her pose, although in a way only an insolent male could manage by crossing his legs at the ankles. "You're in a mood today."

"You scared me, sneaking up like that. Where did you come from?"

"I've been right here the whole time. You're the one who's miles away."

He was dressed just as he was the last time she'd seen him: t-shirt, jeans, and dark leather jacket, giving off that stereotypical bad boy persona. Although his goatee looked to be recently trimmed, and his clothes freshly washed, a weariness shown in his eyes, a look that said he hadn't slept well in some time.

"So, how you getting along, Gracie? Making friends? Settling in?"

"I'm as settled as I need to be."

"That's right," he said with a snap of his fingers. "You're just a temporary fixture here. So, no new friends, then?"

Grace considered Hank's question. Colin had assumed she'd made friends. Allie, Duncan... The people here were certainly more open and welcoming than any she had met before. Well, most of them.

Colin himself had managed to get closer to breaking through her walls than any other in an extremely long time. And as much as Grace fought it, part of her longed to let him succeed.

But the part of her she knew best, the only part she allowed others to see, replied, "I don't want to make friends."

"Yes, you do," Hank retorted with a laugh. "You're just not willing to admit it. You're also afraid."

Grace didn't debate the issue. Instead, she turned, facing away from him to lean on the railing with her elbows. And yet, she didn't stop herself from asking, "Are you a psychologist, Hank?"

"You could say that. Got an undergraduate degree."

She glanced back at him from over her shoulder, wondering if he was serious. His expression gave away nothing.

Hank chuckled. "It doesn't take an expert, Gracie. You're no more mysterious than a pencil."

Blinking, she twisted around to face him, a string of unkind words on the tip of her tongue.

"Hold up," he said, laughter making it hard for him to get the words out. "I didn't mean that the way it sounded. I'm not saying you're simple, only that it's written all over you. It's in your eyes, the expression on your face, and how you hold yourself. Even what you don't say screams what you wish you could."

His words struck like the sting of a whip. That someone, *anyone* other than Father Tim, could see her so clearly was an intrusion on her soul. To know her secret desires, dreams she dared not speak aloud lay exposed for Hank to see—for *anyone* to see—made it difficult to breathe. And yet when she thought about it, Colin often looked at her as though he could see inside her soul as well.

She swallowed, sucked in air, and tried again to reply. "If that's true, tell me, what it is I'm afraid of?"

"Gracie, Gracie, Gracie," Hank repeated with an accentuated shake of his head. "You're afraid of the same things we all are. You're afraid that you'll never find what you're searching for. And you know why?" She shook her head. "Because you believe you don't deserve it.

"See, I know because that's where I went wrong, and in the end, I screwed up royally. But you, Gracie, you've still got a chance. All you have to do now is convince yourself of that and stop fighting it. Have a little faith."

CHAPTER 20

The Chief's warning succeeded in convincing Colin he had made a huge mistake. After leaving the station house, Colin promised himself he would devise a plan and put it into action as quickly as he could manage; Christmas was just around the corner, after all.

Whatever Grace's past, he intended to stand by his woman. Well, not *his* woman... Yet.

So as not to risk losing the war before the battle had even begun—or however that saying goes—he made some calls, and with the help of his father and a few good friends, Colin did some reconnoitering and put things in motion. And now that Pop was back from lunch, it was time to advance the front line.

As Colin headed for the door, he pulled his cell phone from the pocket of his jeans and sent a text.

Leaving now. Give me five minutes.

A cold wind slapped him in the face as he hit the sidewalk at a brisk pace, sending a chill right through him that he barely noticed. He was anxious and yet apprehensive at the same time. He told himself this was for Grace's own good, but the simple truth was, he ached to see her. He couldn't stop imagining what it might be like to hold her in his arms and feel her body pressed snug against his own. He wanted to taste those lips, caress her creamy skin, and whisper all his secret desires in her ear.

But even more, even if a future for them wasn't what the Lord had in mind, he wanted to pull Grace out of her past, to ease her fears, and help her get over the pain, whatever the cause might be.

Because whatever her crimes—most likely nothing more than a misunderstanding—he knew without a doubt that Grace deserved to be forgiven. Even if the only person withholding that forgiveness was Grace herself.

Of course, although he tried not to let his curiosity veer in that direction, he couldn't help but wonder...

No, Colin told himself with an emphatic shake of his head. He wouldn't go there. Whoever Grace St. John had been in the past, it didn't matter. His energy was much better spent trying to understand who she was now, the woman he would get to know, despite her resistance.

Still, something had happened in her past—something that caused her to be so guarded, and he hated to even imagine what, but how could he help her overcome it if not?

Well, with any luck, Colin mused, he'd have answers to those questions and more within the hour.

He'd taken the long way by rounding the block and coming up from Sycamore. This way, Grace wasn't as likely to spot him too soon, and now in place, he watched out of the corner of his eye while loitering on the sidewalk in front of Debbie's Five and Dime. He kept his hands tucked in his pockets—one of them wrapped around his cell phone—and stared into the window as if he found Debbie's holiday display fascinating.

The glass door to Carmine's Barber Shop opened and out stepped Pop's good friend, Zee, who stopped short. "Colin. Fancy finding you out in the middle of the day. Christmas shopping?"

"Afternoon, Zee. No, uh..." Colin's cell phone vibrated, followed by a corresponding ping. He pulled it from his pocket and glanced at the screen. "Just looking," he said, returning his attention to Zee. "I'm on my way to Pat's to grab some lunch."

The door to another storefront swung open, and the sound of a jangling bell pulled both men's attention. Zee glanced over his shoulder, and Colin's gaze followed his to watch Grace exit the bookstore with her head down.

The older man's eyes narrowed as he turned them back toward Colin. "You wouldn't be having lunch with *her*, would you?" Zee asked with a jerk of his thumb in Grace's direction.

Colin heard Zee had been giving Grace a hard time, but this was the first he'd seen any indication of it for himself. He grinned and patted Zee on the shoulder as he started past. "That's the plan, Old Man. See you later."

Colin didn't wait for a retort from his father's good friend; there was no reason to and plenty of reasons he didn't have the time. He hurried down the sidewalk, just managing to grab the handle of the door to Pat's Hoagies at the same time Grace did.

"C–Colin!" she nearly screeched. "What are you doing here?"

He shrugged. "Same thing you are, I'd imagine, grabbing some lunch." Holding back his amusement, he ushered her in before him.

Once inside, the smells of simmering tomato sauce and spicy Italian sausage filled the air, along with wood smoke from a crackling fire in the hearth.

Pat's Hoagies was a kind of mixed bag as far as restaurants go. The original side served as a sort of deli with a meat counter resembling that of a butcher shop. Behind the counter, high up on the wall hung a huge blackboard displaying the sandwich menu, drinks, sides, and assorted desserts. But when the neighboring shoe store closed up shop some years back, Pat purchased the adjoining storefront, allowing him to expand. When he did, he added two dozen tables and four times that number of chairs in dark wood, a stone fireplace, and textured walls that gave the place an authentic Italian villa flavor.

Outside of Grace's vision, as she stared up at the menu board, Colin motioned to Pat, a boisterous man with a thick Italian accent, a big bowl of a belly and dark hair graying at the temples, who gave Colin a wink and a sly nod.

"*Ciao*, Gracie. It's a so good to see you today," Pat's voice boomed as he strode from the kitchen to the front counter with a wide and welcoming grin. "Please a tell me you're eating in today. I've got a special dessert just a for you."

"Um..." she began shooting a sideways glance in Colin's direction. "I'll be eating in, yes, so...sure, I'll give the dessert a try."

"That's a good girl. And what can I get you to go with it?"

"What haven't I tried yet?"

Pat belted out a laugh, then said to Colin, "This girl, she's a stealing my heart and breaking it at the same time. She says she wants to try everything on the menu before she leaves a town. We need a young buck like a you to make her change her mind."

Turning his attention back to Grace, Pat asked, "How about a Chicken Parmesan? The meal, not a sandwich. It's a my special today."

"That sounds great."

"Good, good. Mick, he's a got you already set up by the fire, Gracie. You sit and warm yourself. I'll have that out to you *un attimo*."

"Thank you, Pat." Grace started for the table as the restaurant owner instructed, only to come to an abrupt halt a few feet away.

CHAPTER 21

Colin glanced from her to the rear table set for two, where Mick held out a chair. Colin also noted that the only other tables currently occupied were near the front windows giving them as much privacy as the intimate eatery would allow. He imagined Grace had noted that too because her mouth had tightened into a thin line. But with the good manners she was known to possess, Grace nodded a thank you to the owner's nephew and settled into her seat.

Pat didn't employ a wait staff during weekday lunch hours, only weekends and during dinner starting at four. Otherwise, if you chose to eat in, you ordered at the counter, picked up your meal from there too, and seated yourself. This time of day, it was just Pat and his nephew Mick running the place. Pat was owner, cook, official greeter and cashier, while Mick played sous-chef, busboy, delivery boy, and dishwasher, but never maître d' or waiter. Lucky for Colin that Pat was a romantic at heart and more than willing to lend a hand.

Colin placed his own order then slipped into the chair across from Grace with both their drinks in hand—a tall glass of water for him and for her a steaming cup of hot tea.

"Be careful that cup is hot."

The look Grace gave him was mixed. Not exactly welcoming, but she wasn't running for the door, either. He took the latter as a good sign.

Her lips twisted in a smirk. "Now I get why Allie spent ten minutes in the bathroom claiming to be sick, then all of a sudden she's fine and insisting I take an extra-long lunch."

Colin bit back a grin. "Glad to hear she's feeling better. I hope you'll take her up on the longer lunch. I'm curious about this dessert Pat's made."

"I don't appreciate being tricked, Colin. You could have just called or stopped by the bookstore if you wanted to ask me—"

"Would you have agreed to have lunch with me if I'd asked?"

Grace lowered her gaze.

"I didn't think so."

Sipping from her cup of hot tea, Grace eyed him from over its rim. "Still, you didn't have to go to all this trouble. I explained where and how I found it. There's nothing else I can tell you."

Colin set his glass back down on the table. "Found what?"

"You know."

"No, Grace, I don't know. Tell me."

"*The box*," she said with a bite in her tone. "Isn't that what this is all about?"

"No. What box?"

"The box—" She broke off as Mick set their meals in front of them, but the moment the young man disappeared through the swinging door leading to the kitchen, Grace leaned in and lowered her voice. "The box I handed over to Father Stephen last Wednesday morning. The one I found on the top shelf of the linen closet."

A sense of dread had Colin's stomach churning. "A box filled with something similar to what we came across more than a week ago, I'm guessing. And did this box happen to look like a cigar box?"

Grace nodded. "It was a child's pencil box, 1930s, I think."

She looked directly into his eyes, and he could only imagine the anguish she saw there. "I'm sorry," she said. "You were so upset Sunday night, and I didn't think you'd want me to..." After throwing a surreptitious glance at their fellow diners, Grace lowed her voice

114

even more. "I was as discrete as I could think to be, I promise, and Father Stephen assured me he would get it to your chief of police and explain everything."

Colin mentally added another visit to Chief Daniels to his list of things to do before the day's end. He would also have to make time to have a talk with his father and fill him in on this latest development. But for right now...

"Let's save that conversation for later," he suggested. "By my calculations, we've got approximately forty-seven minutes to learn more about each other, and I don't want to waste a single second."

Grace's gaze became more shuttered than before. "I would have thought you'd learned enough about me already. Besides, there's no purpose—"

"There *is* a purpose, Grace. You had hope, remember?" She opened her mouth, ready to deny it; he could see it on her face and in her eyes, so he stopped her before she could. "Don't you dare. You admitted it, and I'm not letting you take it back."

"Colin—"

"Hush a minute and let me finish." He had to get this out while the getting was good, and he had to make sure he did it right. "All I'm asking is to be able to spend time with you, to get to know you, and for you to get to know me. So, I'm proposing that we strike a deal."

"What kind of *deal?*"

"A simple one, and if you think about it, I'm really only piggybacking on a promise you've already made, so it won't even be that difficult."

Grace's mouth twisted into a frown, and Colin guessed he was going to have to use a little manipulation to get what he wanted.

"You promised Charlie you would work through the holidays, which means we've got three weeks, right?"

"Less than that, actually. Christmas is—"

"I know how many days left until Christmas. I just assumed that included New Year's."

Grace shrugged. "If Charlie needs me, then, of course, I'll stay a few more days, but according to Allie, the bookstore's typically as quiet as church on a Monday that entire week." When he raised a brow in question, she turned a palm up and said, "I quote, 'Everybody confessed their sins on Saturday, got their forgiveness on Sunday and now they have six whole days to let loose.'"

Colin chuckled. "Sounds like something Allie would say."

"You two know each other well, I take it?"

"Pretty well. We both grew up here. Allie was two grades behind me, though."

Grace nodded, and although she didn't ask anything more, he could see the questions in her eyes.

"Okay, so let's just stipulate that the deal holds for as long as you're in St. Thad."

"I still don't know what—"

"The deal is that starting today, we spend time getting to know each other. Uh-huh," he said, jutting a palm out in front of him, "hold that thought and let me finish before you shut me down. It doesn't have to be in the form of a date, just two people who happen to meet up at the same place at the same time and spend that time together doing things like talking over a meal, for example."

Grace sat back in her chair and crossed her arms over her middle. "So, my part of this deal is—"

"Simple. Just don't fight it. If you're available and I'm available, we hang out."

"That's the second time I've heard that in as many days."

"Heard what?"

"Nothing," she said, waving her own comment away. Sitting back in her chair, Grace appeared to be thinking over his proposal as she took a bite of chicken, chewed, swallowed, and patted her mouth with her napkin. After a long minute, she asked, "What if after a couple more hours in my company, you decide you've made a mistake?"

Colin tilted his head. He found it not only interesting but also encouraging that she hadn't asked what if *she* decided them spending time together was a mistake.

He said, "If at any time Party A—meaning whoever is wanting to call it quits—decides they wish to do so, he or she must give notice to Party B, *in person*, and that notice must contain a reason as to why. Party A must then give Party B ample opportunity to talk Party A into changing his or her mind."

Grace narrowed her eyes, but the slight lift at the corners of her mouth gave her away. "Define 'ample opportunity.'"

Colin nearly laughed out loud, but he was smart enough not to. "How's ten minutes sound?"

"Five."

"Fifteen."

Grace blew out a breath. "I just don't see how this is going to work."

"Okay, I see what you're doing here." He put down his fork and took a fortifying gulp of water. "You're playing the part of Party A, which makes me Party B. So, state your reason why you can't finish your lunch with me at the same table?"

She opened her mouth and closed it again, saying nothing and letting another thirty seconds pass before she lowered her head and asked in a hushed voice, "Why? Why do you want to do this? I'm only here for a short time, and besides, you've got enough people in your life to worry about without—"

"See, now, I'm going to consider that receipt of Party A's argument and rebut it with this: Yes, I have a family to worry about. For all intents and purposes, I'm all that Mom and Pop have right now, or at least all they have to rely on. And although the twins have the three of us, those kids are *my* responsibility because last summer, I went to court and got myself appointed as legal guardian. You could also say I have my friends and all the people in this town to look after, too, because if I see a man, woman, or child—hell, add animal or inanimate object to the list—in need of a helping hand, I'm there to give it."

He took a breath before lifting her chin with a finger so she would look him in the eye. "And you, Grace St. John, are a woman in need of a helping hand. That doesn't mean I'm doing this out of pity or sympathy, either, so don't go getting defensive. You're also the only one I can talk to about what you and I both found in that house, and with the chief of police looking into it, I expect to be needing a shoulder to lean on. A shoulder that belongs to someone who doesn't know my brother, so they won't be tempted to come to his defense. It also needs to be someone I can trust not to let this new development get out to the whole town. Mom and Pop don't need that gossip going around, especially not at Christmastime."

Grace swallowed visibly, and judging by the glimmer of moisture in her eyes, Colin suspected he had her. Still, some insurance just in case he was wrong wouldn't hurt.

He added, "That's all over and above the fact that I've wanted to get a taste of you ever since I looked in through your passenger side window. All I'm asking for is a chance to convince you that you want that too."

He paused and huffed out a breath. "I'll promise you here and now that you have nothing to fear from me, Grace; I'll never step over the line with you, as long as you give me that chance, so help me God. Plus," he went on before she could get a word in, "you did say there was something about this town, something about *me* that made you want to try, and that's all I'm asking. Just try.*"*

It took way too long to get a response, but finally, she nodded, and that was good enough for him.

They both tucked into their meals, then the moment Grace opened her mouth to speak, Colin jumped in with, "So, for starters, tell me more about your name and this St. John guy who adopted you."

Grace huffed and set down her fork. "Why do you *always* cut me off?"

Colin lifted a shoulder. "Because it's fun. So, St. John?"

Grace shook her head and laughed, despite her obvious frustration with him. She then stalled by taking another big bite of chicken and savoring it for as long as possible. Following her lead, Colin bit into a plump meatball.

"St. John's Catholic Church," she replied a short while later. "That's where I was disposed of by my birth mother, or whoever thought that was the right thing to do with an infant they didn't want. I didn't come with any identification, and no one ever claimed to know anything about where I came from, so... That's how I got the name."

"Your mother, or whoever could have chosen a much worse alternative."

"I remind myself daily of that fact."

Colin nodded. "And your first name?"

Grace smiled and lifted a shoulder in a half-hearted shrug. "I'm told that I never once cried and always maintained an innate grace even with a dirty diaper."

Colin could tell by the look in her eyes that the memory was a fond one. "I can see it. That grace," he clarified. "My mom chose our names, Camdyn and mine. It's no secret she has a thing for Scots."

Grace let out a quiet laugh. "No, it's definitely not a secret. Is your father Scottish by descent, then?"

"Our surname is Scottish, so I suppose Pop has some Scot in him somewhere along the family line. He was born and raised on a ranch in Wyoming, and that's all the heritage Pop needs far as he's concerned."

"Yet he lives in this out of the way town where tree farming is more prevalent than ranching and runs a hardware store."

Colin took a bite of his calzone as the story he'd heard so many times growing up ran through his mind. About the incredible loss his dad had suffered and the signs that led him to St. Thaddaeus. How the moment Duncan Haney set eyes on Lizbeth Pettyjohn, a petite young blonde with fiery eyes and a sassy spirit, he knew he never wanted to spend another day without her in his life.

"Long story how that happened," Colin replied. "But we've gotten off subject. You said the other night that the man who found you gave you that name, but now you're telling me you're named after a church?" Colin instantly regretted the question as all the pleasure and amusement that had filled her eyes and brightened her face only moments before disappeared.

Grace shook her head and dropped her napkin in her lap. Colin was nothing like Allie, and getting him off track and keeping him there would only work for so long. She'd seen that firsthand the other night and knew better than to give him the opportunity to probe into her past. Yet here she sat.

And besides, if she wasn't honest with him, was that even really trying? With an inward sigh, she mentally raised a fist and marched forward.

"Father Tim was the parish priest. He couldn't have adopted me even had he wanted to."

"I see." Colin nodded his head as if in thought. "What about later when you *were* adopted? No name change?"

She shook her head. "Everyone assumes babies get snatched up for adoption with ease, and it may be that way for the most part, but it's not always that simple. Especially once you end up in the foster care system and your caseworker has a penchant to forget about you."

Grace asked herself how much she would tell him but didn't take the time needed to come to a decision before she started talking again. "I don't remember who fostered me before the age of four, but I do know I was bounced from one home to another more than half a dozen times in those few years. Either caring for an infant or toddler suffering from the effects of drug use during their gestation was more than my foster parents could handle or more than they wanted to.

After that, every place I ended up never lasted very long. Sometimes they chose to get rid of me, and every once in a while, my caseworker would actually do her job. Then there were times I had no choice but to fend for myself," Grace finished, her voice cracking with emotion. She swallowed and was just about to say more when Colin stopped her with a comforting squeeze of her hand.

"I don't even know what to say, Grace. I'm so sorry you had to go through that."

She tossed his pity aside with a lift of her chin and let the soothing heat of her tea clear the lump in her throat.

After a moment, Colin said, "I get the impression you got to know this priest—Father Tim, was it?—while growing up."

Grace refocused the swarming memories, shoving the bad ones back where they belonged and allowing the good to fill her.

She answered with a genuine smile. "They called him my bulldog. He forever kept tabs on me and even made it possible for me to attend parochial school, off and on."

So you see him often?"

"Not as often as I would have liked," she explained, lowering her gaze, "but he's always been there for me in one way or another. He rescued me more than a few times and stood up for me when—" As another bolt of emotion clogged her throat, Colin squeezed her hand again, but Grace didn't allow herself to savor his touch any longer or accept the intimacy he offered.

Just as she pulled away, the jangle of a bell and Pat's booming welcome pulled their attention to the person coming through the door.

The man in uniform glanced around, met Grace's gaze, then instantly moved on to Colin. The officer raised a finger indicating he needed a moment before turning to Pat to place his order, and a minute later strode toward them with purpose.

"Afternoon, Haney."

"Chief," Colin said as he sat back in his seat. "You here to save me a trip?"

After a sideways glance at a group of diners looking their way, the police chief said to Colin, "I'm still having trouble with that outlet in my office and thought maybe you could come by and take another look."

Ignoring the man's implied question, Colin looked over at Grace and made the introductions.

Daniels stuck out a hand. "Welcome to St. Thaddaeus, Miss St. John. The bookstore was next on my list of errands. I wanted to thank you for your delivery the other day; the assistance is greatly appreciated, although I would have preferred to hear it all from you directly."

"I understand that," Grace replied, "but circumstances—"

"I understand the circumstances," the chief interrupted with a staying hand, "so there's no need for you to say more. I just wanted to be sure you didn't feel uncomfortable with the idea of coming to me directly should the need arise again. And as to that, I owe you an apology for any grief my staff or I have caused you. I hope you'll accept that apology as well as my assurance that it won't happen again."

Grace shook her head. "No apology necessary. I'm only here for a short while, so really, what does it matter?"

The officer cleared his throat. "Well, you've got the apology regardless."

Shifting both his weight and his gaze, Chief Daniels dismissed her and returned his attention to Colin. "So, how about it?"

"This afternoon's going to be tough. I'm covering the store for Pop while he installs Mrs. Wilson's new gas stove, then I'm due to pick the twins up from school. How about you just break the news now?"

Daniels threw a glance toward Grace and again shifted from one foot to the other. "According to Bax, the contents of those packages, both what you brought me and what Miss St. John here found match what was taken from the medical clinic."

Colin's mouth thinned. "Did Bax say how much of what was taken is there?"

"Not quite a third."

"Order up!" Mick called out from the counter.

Chief Daniels waved in Mick's direction then turned back to the table. "I know this news seals something in your mind, Haney, but all it does for me is add more questions. You should keep that in mind."

When nobody spoke, the chief turned to Grace. "It was a pleasure meeting you, and thanks again for your assistance." Then, with a tip of his hat, he went to collect his lunch and was out the door.

Grace returned her attention to Colin. His expression was too dour, the look in his eyes too bleak. She wanted to reach over and take his hand; to offer comfort as he had offered her only minutes before. But she was too cowardice to do so, too afraid of rejection, or worse.

She wished she could talk to Father Tim right now, right this minute. She thought of the cell phone in her handbag and itched to take it out. Pulling the image of his number in her contact list to mind, she imagined doing so just like she had at least a thousand times before and could hear the sound of his voice in her head.

"Grace," he used to always say, instead of hello, *"I've been waiting for you to call."*

With a brief close of her eyes, Grace gave herself another stern lecture: *When will you learn to stand on your own?* Then, opening them again, she saw the look on Colin's face, the pain in his eyes, and knew she couldn't walk away.

Leaning into the table, she spoke barely above a whisper. "Chief Daniels is right, you know? There's any number of reasons why those drugs could have been left in the house."

"Oh yeah," Colin said with a snort of derision, "I can think of several." Then raising a hand, he began ticking them off with a finger each. "Possibility number one, Angela was nice enough to split the haul with Cam before she took off. Possibility number two, Cam was nice enough to split the haul with Angela before she took off. Possibility number three, they both agreed to split the haul until they met up again as planned."

CHAPTER 22

Santa Claus beamed from his golden throne, centering the children's area of the small-town bookstore. School had let out an hour earlier, and the jolly elf—Grace had to admit, Zee did play the part well—had just finished his reading of *How Barker Almost Ruined Christmas*.

All the children present, of which there were approximately twenty by Grace's estimation, were as attentive as well-heeled pups for the duration of storytime but were now pumped with energy, their bellies full of sugary snacks and hot chocolate. Half were running amok, zigzagging between shelves and dodging customers, while the other half either sat in small chairs at the few child-sized tables entertaining themselves with a game or puzzle and a few more spread out on the floor using their elbows to prop up their chins, reading.

The week had flown by with long days and evenings spent at the bustling bookstore. Allie typically worked the early morning through mid-afternoon shift, while Grace took late mornings through closing, allowing Allie to spend evenings with her family.

Grace expected this schedule to deter Colin's plan for them to spend time getting to know one another. She'd been wrong.

For the past four days running, she had seen Colin no less than twice daily, and sometimes more. He made a habit of taking a late lunch, allowing him to meet her either at Pat's or Dewley's, where they shared a table and talked non-stop about everything from books and movies to the town and the twins. They even touched on the subject of his brother on a few occasions, but as Grace suspected that was Colin's way of delving into her past, she would strategically divert the subject.

Because her lunch breaks were so late in the day, Colin typically had to cut their time short so he could pick the twins up from school, but would then make up for it by bringing them to the bookstore where they would socialize with friends while he did the same.

Grace shook her head and stifled a grin as she wondered again how the man managed to always find a way to pull her into a conversation with whoever he happened to be conversing with.

Twice now, Colin and the twins had also met her for dinner. Neither time had been planned beforehand, and Grace still hadn't gotten out of him how he'd arranged it. But as those few hours with the three of them had been the most fun Grace could ever remember having, she didn't bother to ask.

Over the course of these last several days, she discovered Alec and Ainsley were happy children, full of good humor, fun-spirited, and the best behaved five-year-olds she had ever met.

Grace also learned that Colin was genuinely a gregarious sort, forever joking, always teasing, cheerful, and laid back. Or that's what he portrayed in public. But when they spoke in hushed tones over a shared table, and the subject of his brother came up, he allowed Grace to see the side of him she had met that night when he'd come to fix the sink. The side that cared deeply for the people around him and the side burdened with guilt over his brother's desertion. That part of him who hid nothing and exposed his true feelings. The part of him that Grace couldn't deny she found both appealing and hard to resist.

That last thought brought back the promise Colin had weaseled out of her earlier today and had Grace glancing up at the clock on the wall. She blew out a hearty sigh just as Allie came up behind her.

"Fifteen minutes to go, and you're out of here. Good thing our shifts had already been switched today," Allie exclaimed, "otherwise you wouldn't have been able to accept the Haneys' invite. And I'm glad you did, don't get me wrong, but I'm also a little put out that you did after refusing all of mine."

Grace snorted a laugh. "Don't be because I haven't given up on devising a way out of it."

"Why?" Allie asked, playfully smacking Grace's arm. "The Haneys are good people. It's not as if you don't know them, and you'll have Alec and Ainsley there for support, too."

"I know. Those two are the only reason I haven't already backed out. The twins are so excited about me coming to see this famous fifty-foot Christmas tree." Her shoulders drooped, and she blew out a breath. "I suppose a party with a hundred people is better than an intimate family dinner."

Allie scoffed. "First off, that tree isn't an inch over twenty feet, and second, the Haneys' annual tree-trimming party is always a hit, but I sincerely doubt there'll be more than forty people max in attendance and you've probably already met every one of them. And don't forget, Charlie and I will be there as soon as we close up."

Grace hesitated, but Allie made it too easy to open up. Too easy to forget she was supposed to be guarding herself against getting too close.

So, Grace gave in. "I don't know how to socialize on that level, and besides, it's been a very long time since I've been in someone's home. It's a vulnerable position to be in, and I don't particularly enjoy putting myself there."

Allie's gaze filled with concern. She relieved herself of the stack of books she had been replacing on the shelves and pulled Grace deeper into a corner.

Lowering her voice, she said, "Honey...I don't know even a tenth of what you've gone through in your life as you haven't really let me in—no, I don't need you to tell me why" she said when Grace opened her mouth to speak "I'm just pointing that out because I want you to know that although I don't know the kind of hurts you've experienced in the past, I can assure you that no one in St Thaddaeus is going to add to that.

"And you'll be fine," Allie went on. "Virginia May and her niece Mac will be there. Mac's your age, and she's always a hoot."

"And Zee," Grace added with a frown.

Allie laughed out loud. "Yes, I have no doubt he'll be there. He is the Mayor of St. Thad, after all."

"Mayor? I had no idea," Grace said with a sniff. "That isn't saying much for what should be this town's official welcoming committee."

"True," Allie agreed with a hint of pink tinging her cheeks. "But if you ask me, Zee's coming around. I've hardly heard a grumble out of him the past couple of days."

"Maybe. But he still throws a sneer my way every now and then."

"I've seen that, and have you noticed that whenever he does, and someone else notices, they make a point of coming over to you just to say hi and ask how you're doing? It's like giving Zee a kick in the pants. That should tell you something."

A quiet giggle escaped before Grace could hold it back. "It does, and I'll admit that every time it happens, I'm tempted to act like one of those five-year-olds and stick my tongue out at him."

Allie shook her head. "I just can't figure out why he's been acting this way toward you; I've never known Zee to have a problem with anyone new to town."

"Obviously, because it's me, in particular. I keep assuring him I'm only here for a few more weeks. You'd think that would be enough to satisfy him."

Allie tilted her head in thought. "Maybe that *is* the problem."

"What do you mean?"

"Maybe instead of constantly reminding everyone that you're leaving, you ought to start thinking about staying."

When Grace didn't instantly reply, Allie snatched the opportunity to say more. "I know you don't have anywhere, in particular, you need to be; that much you've told me. And I also know you're not on your way to see family, otherwise, why would you be spending this time of year all alone?

"Whether you intended to or not, Grace, you've made connections in St. Thad, and you should really think about what it will mean to lose that. Besides missing out on having a great friend like me who will always have your back, think about the other possibilities," she said with a wicked wiggle of her brows.

Grace laughed, and Allie continued. "Colin Haney is a good man; one of the best by my standards, and he's pretty hot for you, Grace, as are those two kiddos over there," she added nodding in the direction where Alec and Ainsley sat at a small table, occupied with a puzzle. "Colin doesn't deserve you turning your back on what he's offering without at least considering it, don't you think?"

Tears welled in Grace's eyes, and a lump formed in her throat so thick that she couldn't have spoken even if she did know what to say.

Allie gave her hand a reassuring squeeze. "Now, as for this party tonight, there's no way I'm going to let you back out. You'll have friends there, and the Haneys are excellent hosts. I guarantee you won't feel vulnerable for long, if at all. Colin will see to that."

"Fine," Grace sighed, ruffling the curls that had escaped her ponytail and now fell over her brow. She appreciated Allie's quick turnabout, allowing her to regain her composure.

"I would have liked to go home and change first, but then Lizbeth asked Duncan to pick up a few last things she needed for the party, which left Colin to close the hardware store. Then the twins didn't want to miss storytime, so I stupidly volunteered to keep an eye on them for a while, and now there's no time."

"Well, this isn't some big, fancy shindig; what you're wearing now is just fine."

Grace glanced down at her conservative gray slacks, matching silk top and plum-colored sweater. Pulling the edges of the open sweater around her like a hug, she shivered. "'Just fine' will have to do, I guess."

"Tell you what. It's getting pretty quiet in here, why don't you let me keep an eye on the twins while you go freshen up? You'll feel more confident once you brush your hair and put a little color in your cheeks."

"I look that bad, huh?" Grace cupped her face.

"No," Allie replied with a snort of laughter. "Matter-of-fact, you look great as always, which is one more reason for me to be put out. But even if it does nothing for you, I'll feel better if you at least give the *illusion* that you had to put a little effort into it."

Allie's perpetual grin and always-present mischievous glint in her eyes softened. "One more thing, Grace. You've been dating Colin for—"

"No, I haven't! We are not dating. I do not date. I made that clear to him from the get-go, as well as the fact that in another two weeks, I'll be gone, so..."

Plopping down into one of those child-sized chairs with a heavy sigh, Grace leaned forward with her elbows on her knees and propped her chin up with the palms of her hands. "I enjoy being with him. He's funny and easy to talk to. I never feel pressured or judged. Never like he's pushing me in a direction I'm not willing to go. You know what I mean?"

Allie slid a second plastic chair in front of Grace, covered her hands with her own, then gave the backs of Grace's hands a pinch.

"Ow! What was that for?"

"That was my way of saying, *wake up*! Deal with reality, Sister. I hear the flutters in your voice that start about thirty minutes before you know you're going to see him. I've seen the way you light up when he walks in here and the way he looks at you, too. And I've noticed how you practically melt into a puddle whenever he touches you. Which he does a lot, by the way. Charlie's noticed, too, and so have others."

Grace sucked in her bottom lip and nibbled.

Allie leaned closer. "Has Colin kissed you yet?" Grace shook her head, and Allie sniffed with disappointment. "I figured not. Do you want him to?"

Grace hesitated then nodded, and Allie patted her hand before giving it another pinch.

"*Ow*! Dammit, Allie, that hurt."

"Good. And if you come in here tomorrow and tell me he still hasn't kissed you, I'll do it again, only harder."

CHAPTER 23

Thanks to the Haney twins, Grace hadn't been given a moment to feel awkward on the way to the party. From the time Colin picked the three of them up at the bookstore and during the entire drive to his parents' house, neither Alec nor Ainsley had stopped talking. Between regaling today's Pulaski boys antics and the twins' bouncing up and down with excitement over their anticipation of helping to decorate the huge spruce their Uncle Colin had helped cut down and set up last night, all Grace had to do was listen and enjoy which she did with continuous bouts of laughter that had tears leaking from the corners of her eyes.

Every now and again, she would glance over at Colin, who was keeping a sharp eye on the road as the weather had turned, bringing colder temperatures along with a dusting of snow that made for icy pavement. Sometimes, when she looked his way, she would see a broad grin on his face accompanied by an occasional laugh, but she suspected by the intermittent frowns and the sadness she saw in his eyes that not all of Colin's thoughts were with them tonight. Something was on his mind, and she couldn't help wondering what.

When they arrived at his parents' place, the first thing Colin did was give her a tour of the sprawling ranch-style home—she should have guessed that would be the case—ending with the great room and the yet unadorned tree where the ceiling was high, the room spacious, and the furnishings chunky, masculine, and sink-into-comfortable.

The walls and tabletops were covered with framed family photos, yet not one depicted their oldest son or the twins' mother.

Since the other guests had yet to arrive, and they were currently alone in the room, Grace snagged the opportunity given. "I imagine the holidays are hard for your parents. Not knowing."

Colin transferred his gaze from a photograph of the twins' first day of school to Grace with a sigh. "Every day is hard, but yeah, the holidays are worse. I hate that Mom and Pop can't display pictures of their oldest son because they're worried the daily reminder that he left will emotionally damage his kids. I hate that they can't mourn because they don't know what they're mourning, a child who's damaged and lost or one who just doesn't give a damn."

It was so tempting to brush her fingers through his thick, silky hair. To offer comfort Grace wasn't sure she even knew how to give. "I get the feeling there's a reason why you blame yourself for your brother's choices, something you haven't said."

Colin glanced toward the kitchen, then over at the twins who were running in circles around the tree, louder than ever, falling over each other and laughing uncontrollably.

They had been talking quietly from their semi-secluded spot a good twenty feet away, but Colin lowered his voice even more, speaking barely above a whisper. "I knew Cam had been experimenting with drugs. I caught him and his friends in the bathroom at school. We were only one grade apart, so..." He shrugged as if the incident had meant nothing. "Anyway, after that, it was easy to tell when Cam would show up at my games or come home lit. I knew, and I didn't say a word to anyone. I never even tried to talk to Cam about it, not even when he left for California."

"And you think telling someone, saying something to your brother would have made a difference?"

"Yeah, I do. We were close before that. I could have at least tried. I might have been able to talk some sense into him."

****

Shortly after the party got in gear, Lizbeth recruited Grace to man a station at the children's craft table where kids of all ages were already busy making ornaments.

Lizbeth set her up with a full plate of *hors d'oeuvres* and a generous snifter of spiced eggnog, while Duncan made sure the flock of children in attendance knew where to find her. She suspected Colin had put his parents up to it knowing she felt much more comfortable with the younger humans than she did with those in the double digits.

She had been at it for nearly an hour now, and although there always seemed to be a handful of adults hovering nearby, Grace never felt crowded or vulnerable as she expected she would. And, although Colin had been pulled away by one person or another on numerous occasions, he continually came back to stand by her side.

With that thought in mind, Grace realized she hadn't seen him in a while. After handing a reindeer constructed of paper and a cotton ball nose off to the giddy child who made it, Grace slid her gaze toward the twenty-foot spruce draped in multi-colored blinking lights, and already half-filled with ornaments of every shape and size. While most of the guests seemed more than happy to stand back and watch the bevy of activity taking place around the tree, others lifted giggling children in the air so they could attach handmade ornaments to high hanging branches, and still more adults carefully arranged those ornaments that were not necessarily more cherished but most definitely more breakable. She saw both Ainsley and Alec mixed within that bunch, and Duncan as well, but no Colin.

"Okay, Grace, time's up. I'm here to relieve you."

Grace jumped at the familiar voice as she hadn't seen Mackenzie's approach. She put a hand to her racing heart before flicking one more glance out into the room.

Mac handed her a refill of spiced eggnog. "If you're looking for Colin, he's over there," she said with a negligent wave of her hand.

Glancing in the direction Mac indicating, Grace finally caught sight of Colin's dark head, standing near the stone fireplace.

He appeared to be deep in conversation, a serious one judging by the expression on his face, as he leaned an elbow on the wooden mantel with a glass of eggnog in one hand and the other wrapped around the fingers of a striking brunette.

Grace didn't recognize the woman as anyone she knew, but their body language told her that clearly, Colin did. He was standing close enough that it would have taken no effort at all for him to lean in and press his mouth to hers.

The woman was dressed in a slinky black sheath, one of those to-die-for cocktail dresses that every woman needed to have at least one of in her closet. Her thick wavy hair fell to the middle of her back, and when she turned her head, Grace saw that her big brown eyes had been made up with an expert hand, and her lips were full, lush and siren red. Even the hint of a tiny dimple at the corners of her mouth were worth despising her over.

From Grace's side, Mac smirked. "Faith's gorgeous, isn't she? I don't know about you, but just looking at her makes me want to rip her phenomenal hair out."

Grace focused on the bow she was supposed to be tying around a glitter-covered Styrofoam ball. Once secure, she handed the ornament back to a child, who gleefully ran off to add it to the Christmas tree.

In a tone she hoped didn't give anything away, Grace said, "Must be a good friend, I'm guessing, someone Colin went to school with? They seem familiar."

That comment earned another snort from Mac. "Cozy, you mean. Yeah, he and Faith dated in high school. Nothing serious, of course, they were just kids. Faith left for college right after graduation, and less than a year later, we heard she was married and already knocked up. Her oldest is eight! Can you believe that body has given birth to three kids?"

Mac shook her head. "Anyway, she moved back to St. Thad about two years ago after her husband was killed. Military. Which I guess makes me a real B-I-T-C-H," she whispered, "for being so catty, but can you blame me? Lord knows I didn't need the competition."

Mac ended her rant with another sneer in the couple's direction, which had Grace staring at Mac with surprise.

"I'm not talking about *Colin*, in particular," Mac said with a wrinkle of her nose, "I mean competition in general. *Geez*, Grace, if I wanted Colin Haney all to myself, I would have run you out of town a week ago."

Grace couldn't help it, she laughed and gave Mac's shoulders a squeeze. Then, with another glance toward Colin who hadn't moved, she said to Mac, "If you're taking over here, I think I'll go find the restroom before I say goodnight."

"You're leaving? It's not even eight o'clock."

"I know, but I have to be at the bookstore early tomorrow, and I'm a bit tired already; it's been a long day."

She said her goodbyes to Mackenzie then wove her way through the crowd and down a long hallway where Lizbeth had pointed out the nearest bathroom.

Hanging her head over the sink, Grace berated herself for acting like no less of a B-I-T-C-H than Mac had. She had no right to be jealous, and certainly no right to be mad. She had told Colin from the onset that she had every intention of leaving at the end of the month. Still, here she was, fighting back angry tears, which just made her even madder.

She splashed cold water on her face, straightened her shoulders, and pulled open the door, only to come face-to-face with Virginia, the B&B owner.

"Grace! Goodness, you startled me."

"Sorry."

"Oh, no bother. It's my own fault, really; I'd already had my hand on the doorknob. Anyway, I'm glad I found you. Little Alec was looking all over for you. He wants to make one of those sleds made out of popsicle sticks, and Mac has no idea how it's done. She's hoping you could show her before you leave."

Grace had gotten a glimpse of the twins' competitive nature and didn't want to leave Alec without at least a chance to match his sister's efforts, so she hurried back to the craft table.

About halfway through her detailed instructions, Colin came up behind her and laid a gentle hand on her arm. Although Grace had already scolded herself for the emotions churning in her gut and thought she had been working her way past it pretty well, the thrill of his touch ignited something sour, and before she could dispel the emotion, she shrugged him off.

Colin's head tilted as he narrowed his eyes. "I wanted to introduce you to someone."

Determined to make up for the impulsive slight, Grace turned with a forced smile on her face that disappeared the second she saw the sleek brunette at his side.

"Grace, this is Faith Daws–uh, Pulaski. We went to school together. Faith, this is Grace St. John, the woman your boys have been crushing on for the past couple of weeks."

Faith stuck out her hand, which Grace ignored. The woman's laugh sounded real, and her smile appeared genuine, but Grace was in no mood to be pleasant.

"It's so good to finally meet you," Faith cooed, her voice just as silky and sexy as her outfit. "I've been wanting to make it down to the bookstore but just haven't been able to work it into my schedule. I was telling Colin that all I hear these days during dinner and bedtime rituals is 'Grace did this' and 'Grace said that.' Joshua's the quiet one, but Jesse and Jordan have already had a few mock battles over who gets to claim your affections."

"I supposed I've overstepped—" Grace began.

"Oh, I doubt you have, but please, overstep all you want. They're good boys at heart, but can be a handful when not within my sight." With a flirty bat of her eyes and a wink directed at Colin who grinned in return, Faith added, "Colin was just lecturing me on the importance of having a father-figure in their life."

Grace felt the sting of that shared look all the way to her toes. Turning to the two-timing scum, she said, "I was just on my way to find your parents so I could say goodnight and thank them—"

"Grace!" Colin's lips thinned on the single word, which had come out sharp and scolding in tone. Grace blinked in surprise, and for several long seconds, no one in their small circle said another word. Faith's mouth dropped open, and beside her, Mac cleared her throat.

As heat singed Grace's cheeks, Colin wrapped his fingers around hers and took hold. "Excuse us," he said as he turned and dragged Grace away, pulling her through the house.

CHAPTER 24

He headed for the kitchen but didn't stop there. With a nod to his mother, he snatched a napkin filled with crab rolls off a tray and continued right on into the laundry room where he came just short of slamming the door behind them.

They were immediately engulfed in darkness while he fumbled to find the light switch. His arm brushed along her breast, sending a jolt of electricity straight to his crouch and causing Grace to gasp in surprise.

When the light came, on he blinked at the sudden glare as he watched Grace do the same.

Everything in Colin screamed to tell her how he felt, to take her into his arms as he'd been wanting to do all week and pull her inside. But the moment he had extended the invite to tonight's party, he could sense that barrier he'd fought so patiently to break down this week being erected again.

He figured it was the fear that he was already losing her that had him striking out in anger, but he didn't take the time to analyze it.

"Okay, spill it. What's wrong with you?"

Grace scowled in response. "What's wrong with me? What's wrong with you?"

"Don't you dare turn this around. Why were you so rude to Faith, and why do you want to leave all of a sudden?"

"I wasn't rude, and it's not all of a sudden. I'd already told Mac I had to go—"

"You were and is so." Colin winced at his own words. *I've been spending way too much time with five-year-olds.* "Right before we walked up, you were all smiles and enjoying yourself."

"Maybe like someone else I know I was faking it."

Colin narrowed his eyes. "I suppose that someone is supposed to be me?"

"If the Santa hat fits..."

Stunned by the flash of anger in her eyes, and the instantaneous panic she had aroused in him, Colin sighed and bowed his head. He had to get himself under control and salvage the situation quickly, but how?

Seconds ticked as he racked his brain, then a snicker diverted his attention. As he lifted his head, that snicker became a snort of laughter.

Following Grace's gaze, he saw that he'd crushed the crab rolls in his fist. He shook his head, dropped the napkin now filled with mush onto the top of the dryer, took a deep breath, and tried again.

"Don't leave, Grace. I've been looking forward to tonight all week."

She raised a brow. "You told me you just remembered this party was tonight when you got up this morning."

"I lied. I didn't want to risk inviting you until I was at least sixty percent certain you'd say yes."

She did a poor job of trying to hide her grin by biting her bottom lip, which gave Colin hope that even more honesty would save the day. "So, let's start again. Tell me why you want to leave."

She sighed. "I don't really, and I *was* having a good time, it's just... When I saw you..."

"Saw me?"

She crossed her arms over her middle. "To use Mac's words, I was being catty," she mumbled.

A moment later, Grace lifted her chin and straightened her shoulders. "I had no right to feel slighted, and I'll apologize to your friend as soon as you let me out of here."

Colin made a point of looking around as if just realizing where they were. He grinned. "Actually, I've been wanting to get you alone for days now, and I'd say this counts." He leaned back against the washing machine and stuffed a bite of crab mush between his lips.

As he chewed, he offered some to Grace, which she declined. He swallowed and wiped his mouth. "So. Catty, huh?"

Grace nodded.

"So, when you say you felt 'slighted,' what you really mean is you were jealous."

She hesitated then nodded again.

"You know, you were wrong earlier? When you said you had no right, you were wrong."

"No," she replied with an adamant shake of her head, "we're not even dating, and besides that—"

"The hell we're not." His words carried no heat whatsoever—the burn was all internal, and he paused, giving Grace time to come to terms with the facts before going on. "I lied there too only because I knew you wouldn't agree to the deal otherwise. But as far as I'm concerned, we're on date number twelve, which by high school standards means we're already going steady."

Grace laughed and shook her head. "I think the concept of 'going steady' disappeared long before either of us was born."

"Maybe where you come from, but here in St. Thaddaeus, it's alive and well."

"You have no idea how to carry on a serious conversation, do you? You're always teasing—"

"I may be teasing, but I'm also dead serious. And seeing as we're going steady," he said, taking her hand in his and slowly pulling her closer, "I think it's high time you let me kiss you."

Her eyes widened, the thrill he saw in them encouraging him even more. "Can I, Grace? Will you let me taste you?"

"I've wanted you to so many times." Her words were barely more than a whisper. Colin held his breath for several beats, watching the emotions churn in her eyes.

He still didn't know the details of her past and was determined to tread carefully. He'd worked hard to earn her trust these past days and would continue to do so by giving her as much time as she needed.

He just prayed she would come around before it was too late.

Finally, she stepped closer of her own volition, and Colin let out the breath he'd been holding. After several more beats, her lips parted and lifted toward his, her eyes closed, and her fists clenched.

With an internal *tsk*, Colin shook his head and grinned.

Taking both her hands, he placed them on his shoulders, and her eyes flew open, the silver flecks now nearly invisible amid the passion that filled the green depths.

He brushed the tips of his fingers through her loose curls, down her temples to her chin, then gently cupped her cheeks.

Keeping his movements slow and as non-threatening as he could manage, he leaned in and touched his lips to her forehead before sliding them down to her cheek, then gently dabbing at the corners of her mouth. The strangled sound she made urged him on.

With slow, gentle strokes, he tasted her lips with his tongue before whisking his mouth over hers from side to side and back again.

Grace moaned as the palms of her hands gripped his shoulders, and she leaned into his touch, igniting the fire between them.

That was all Colin needed; the acceptance and surrender. He gave her his mouth fully then, sharing every ounce of desire he possessed.

She tasted like heaven, and with her mouth moving so eagerly under his Colin discovered that holding back with her was the most difficult thing he'd ever attempted.

Still, he kept his touch light and his hands gentle as he slid them down to her shoulders then skimmed the sides of her breasts.

She opened, and his tongue surged inside, tasting more of her, giving her more of him. She whimpered, and everything in him clenched with desire.

He moved just a little closer, applied a tad more heat and a touch more passion—

Grace broke the kiss and bolted backward, nearly stumbling in her haste.

Her breathing was ragged, her eyes big and filled with regret as she raised a fist to her lips. "I'm sorry. I'm so sorry, Colin, but I can't."

"Grace, if... If someone hurt you, we'll work through it. I can wait—"

She shook her head. "That's not it. I don't have a problem with that. The kiss was great, but it shouldn't have happened. I shouldn't have let you talk me into this *deal* thing in the first place. It makes no sense when I'm leaving in two weeks."

Colin sighed. "Okay, here we go. Party A," he said, pointing a stiff finger toward Grace, "Party B," he finished stabbing his own chest. "Are you done?"

Her lips thinned. She folded her arms over her middle, huffed out a breath, and leaned back against the dryer.

Colin took that as a yes. "Good. My turn. I'll even set the timer," he added, pulling his cell phone from his pocket. Grace sputtered a laugh and grabbed it out of his hands, which he held up in surrender.

"So, before I give you my rebuttal, I want to make sure I understand your argument. Your argument is you're leaving in two weeks. Is that right?"

"Yes."

"And is that the extent of your argument, or is there more?"

She opened her mouth and closed it again.

"Okay, fine. That makes my rebuttal just as simple. The deal was we continue hanging out, getting to know one another for as long as you're in St. Thaddaeus. And you just admitted that you plan to be here for *at least* another two weeks. Another part of the deal was that Party A had to present a valid reason why the deal should be broken, and you, my stubborn girl, have presented none."

She opened her mouth again, and he cut her off. "*And*, I want to add that you also admitted that the kiss was 'great,' that was your word, and if given a chance, I can do a hell of a lot better than *great*. Therefore, I submit to the court that it's only fair I'm given that chance. Unless you'd rather I went back out there and found Faith..."

Grace gasped, and Colin laughed. "I rest my case," he said, and with a bow of her head, Grace dropped her arms to her sides in surrender.

Pressing his body to hers and wrapping his arms around her in a warm embrace, Colin applied a soft kiss to her temple. "Won't you give yourself this gift, Grace? Even if only for a short time, won't you allow yourself to accept what I'm offering, what *we're* all offering? Won't you trust me not to betray you?"

With a whimper, her arms encompassed his waist, and her mouth sought his. Colin didn't hesitate. He took what she offered and dove in. Devouring, drinking in her essence, and giving her all of his. Tasting, sipping, savoring her flavor topped with a hint of spiked eggnog.

His hands roamed her form, brushing the sides of her breasts, the shape of her hips and thighs, and around to skim the length of her spine.

He sucked in a breath as Grace's warm hands found their way beneath his sweater to glide over his bare skin, around his waist and over his back to explore, test, and mold every aching muscle.

He pulled her in, deepening the kiss, his hips and tongue moving in a rhythm as old as time, a dance he longed to share with her over and over again, for as long as she would allow.

A knock on the laundry room door had them breaking apart with sudden clarity. The door opened, and his father cleared his throat before peeking in with a sheepish expression of his face.

"Uh, sorry to interrupt, but your mother told me where to find you."

"No problem, Pop. What's up?"

"The children have been rounded up by the hearth, and they're waiting for their Christmas story. Charlie's here, and he offered, but the Pulaski boys aren't having it. They're threatening to organize a posse and go in search of Grace, so I thought maybe I'd head 'em off at the pass."

She giggled and shook her head. "Now, I see where Colin gets it."

CHAPTER 25

The next six days were a blur of activities. In between the long hours put in at the bookstore, conversations with Hank in the park to and from, and falling into bed each night exhausted, Grace spent every available hour with Colin and most often the twins as well. In addition to shared lunches, dinners, and trips for ice cream, there was church on Sunday, the school Christmas pageant, the town tree lighting, a parade of lights around town square, gingerbread houses, sled races, and snowman building.

On top of all that, the kids were now out of school until after the first of the year and each day since, Barkers' Books hosted morning and afternoon storytime sessions, followed by a choice of coloring, crafting or gift wrapping, and all of it was supervised by Grace.

Except today.

Today was her day off, and instead of spending the day restless and alone as she was well accustomed to, Grace had plans. Big plans that she was both looking forward to and apprehensive about at the same time.

Colin had arranged to also take the day off as he needed to finish his Christmas shopping. The twins were spending most of the day with their Nana, then enjoying a Christmas movie marathon and sleepover with Colin's good friend, Faith, and her three rambunctious boys.

"Where are we going?" Grace asked as she slid into the front seat of Colin's Ford Explorer.

"Steamboat Springs. Shouldn't take longer than two hours, but we'll stop at Dewley's and pick up some hot coffee and a few of Virginia's pastries for the road. Unless you want breakfast."

"No, I'm good."

With a nod, Colin leaned over and placed a soft kiss on her lips. "Good morning."

"Good morning." Heat infused her cheeks, and she turned to reach for her seatbelt, and Colin got them on their way.

"Oh, I almost forgot," he said, lifting an envelope from his center console and handing it to Grace. "Mom asked me to give that to you."

Grace flipped the envelope end over end then brushed the tips of her fingers over her name written in bold red ink. "What is it?"

"Well, in case you haven't heard, Lizbeth Haney is not your typical female—and I don't mean this to sound as sexist as it's going to—but not only does Mom dislike shopping malls, she also loathes shopping online. Inside that envelope, you will find a credit card and shopping list. I've been instructed to tell you that she fully expects you to find everything on that list, and we're not to come home until you do, and you're not to concern yourself with the cost. If you have any questions, her cell number is in there too."

It took Grace a moment to find her voice. "Your mother trusts me to shop for her?"

"Of course. Why wouldn't she?"

"Well, for one thing, she barely knows me."

Colin chuckled. "She likes and trusts you, Grace. That's all she needs to know."

Grace didn't know what to say to that, so she said barely a word for some time.

They stopped at Dewley's to stock up with sugar and caffeine, then headed for the highway where the scenery whizzing by them was filled with little more than snow-covered mountains, vast expanses of evergreens, and the peace of nature.

They fell into a comfortable silence with Colin humming to the Christmas music playing on the radio while Grace fidgeted with the envelope in her hands. They had traveled nearly fifty miles before she opened it.

Grace,

You have no idea how thrilled I am that you're able to accompany Colin today, and not just because I suspect he'll need help with his shopping as well.

Included is a list of the few gifts I have yet to acquire to complete my Christmas list. My only requirement is that you follow the guidelines I've outlined. Other than that, as Colin was instructed to tell you, I don't want to see either of you back in St. Thad until <u>every</u> item on the list has been secured.

I have full faith in your taste and good judgment, and you're only to call if you run into a situation where you can't decide between this or that and need a third opinion.

Merry Christmas,
Lizbeth

P.S. This credit card has a zero balance and a limit well beyond what you'll need, so no being frugal.

Grace couldn't help but laugh. "I see you get your humorous nature from both parents."

Colin glanced her way and grinned. "Oh, yeah? What does it say?"

"Not much more than you already passed on, really. It's just the way she says it."

Grace flipped to the accompanying page and continued reading.

For Ainsley

A doll with several additional outfits. Also, make sure she has long hair that Ainsley can brush and style.

For Alec

A military camo outfit, equipped with helmet, vest, exploding grenades, binoculars, compass, the works. If you have to purchase everything separately, so be it. As long as Alec has what he needs so that his battles with those Pulaski boys are a fair match. And keep in mind, Faith's boys come fully-armed!

For Duncan

My husband needs a new hat and Colin knows just the store and what his dad likes.

For Colin

I need several things for my boy, and only you, Grace, can help me here, so I'm counting on you. My son has had two very long and very hard years. With no warning, he lost a brother and became a father, and since then, he has worked 24/7, giving everything he has to those around him and never taking for himself. Until you.

And now, after watching him these past weeks, I know exactly what gift I want to give him.

Colin needs time off, and I've arranged for him to have the next thirty or so hours. One day and one night of no worries, with time to enjoy the company of a woman he cares for.

I want him to spend hours browsing the shops on Main Street where he can stop and eat when and wherever he wants, and stuff himself with anything other than chicken nuggets or mac and cheese. In fact, you should steer him toward some place where those items are not even on the menu!

However, keep in mind that I've made a reservation for two at his favorite restaurant for 7:00 p.m. sharp—Colin knows the one—and you'll want to show up with an appetite.

I've also reserved a two-bedroom suite at the ski resort Colin has stayed at before—again, he'll know the place—with a three o'clock check-in.

Now, I know neither of you planned to stay overnight, and I doubt you were expecting dinner at a fancy restaurant, either, so I'm <u>ordering</u> you both to purchase whatever you need and put it on this card!

Again, Grace, I'm counting on you. My son deserves this more than anyone I know, and if he comes home having missed out on even one of these small gifts, I'll hold you personally responsible.

Oh, and Charlie isn't expecting you any earlier than noon tomorrow, so make sure my son gets to sleep in.

Yours,
Lizbeth

CHAPTER 26

"Mmm," Grace moaned as she savored her last bite. "That is hands down *the* best Tiramisu I have ever tasted."

"Don't tell Pat. He'll be adding it to his menu, adjusting the recipe, and feeding it to you daily until you swear his is better."

Grace laughed. "I'm sure he would."

It had been easier to pull Grace into the day than Colin predicted. She'd spent the first half of their morning drive in near silence, but after damaging her ears with his renditions of "Jingle Bells," "Silver Bells," and for his finale, "Jingle Bell Rock," he'd had her laughing so hard she was begging for mercy.

From across a candle-lit table, he took a long moment to admire the deep V of the emerald-green wrap dress he'd picked out for her at a local boutique. The color brought out the green of her eyes and showed off her curves. For him, Grace had chosen brown dress pants and a matching brown button-down shirt with thin gold strips that she said enhanced the caramel sheen in his hair.

By 5:45, they had purchased everything on their lists, leaving them just enough time to dump it all in their rooms before hurrying to shower and change for dinner. Now, they had only themselves and their own pleasure to focus on for the rest of their evening.

She asked, "When you checked with the twins earlier, what movie did they say they were watching?"

"Die Hard, I think. Or maybe it was *Die Hard 2."*

"I thought they were going to watch Christmas movies."

Colin gave her his best shocked and disgruntled expression. "I'll have you know, the first two *Die Hard* movies are classic Christmas tales, just as "*Trains, Planes, and Automobiles* is a Thanksgiving staple."

Grace used her napkin to try and hide her grin as she shook her head. "Well, still... *Die Hard?*"

He laughed. "Don't worry, Faith swears it's the TV version; the curse words have been dubbed out."

"That wasn't exactly what I was thinking about. And poor Ainsley—she must have been outvoted."

"Oh, don't worry about the future, Madam President. She got first pick, and they started their movie marathon with *Home Alone.* Now *that* gives me the chills," he added with a mock shiver that had Grace busting out in laughter. "Anyway, I guarantee you Ainsley's having a blast, and while the boys are watching Bruce blow things up, she and Faith are giving each other pedicures, manicures, and facials."

Grace leaned forward with an elbow on the table, her chin propped in the palm of her hand. "Do you ever resent it? The responsibility."

"Not for a single second. I resent my brother for what he's done to our parents and those kids. Knowing that both their mother and father were selfish, undisciplined, and irresponsible people who chose I don't know what over them is something those children are going to have to live with their entire lives. I can only pray that the love and security I give them will be enough to combat the hurt of that."

He looked into her eyes. "I'm so sorry you didn't have that, Grace. God knows you deserved to. No child deserves less."

She nodded and sat back. "I'm sorry I brought it up. I guess I was just thinking about your mother's note. She's very proud of you, and it shows. The twins are incredibly lucky to have all three of you."

"Thanks." He wanted to tell her that she could have all five of them and that the Haneys had more than enough love in them to share. But he knew Grace wasn't ready to hear it quite yet, so he kept that one desire to himself.

He tossed his napkin on the table, stood, and held out a hand. "What do you say we go enjoy some Baileys and coffee in front of that fireplace waiting for us back at the condo?"

****

Staring back at Grace from the full-length mirror was a stranger. An illusion of innocence and seduction dressed in pale pink satin and lace chosen by the man she had foolishly fallen for the moment she opened herself to the possibility.

And when was that? she wondered. When did she make a conscious choice to give in, or had she at all?

Was it as they raced down Anael Hill side by side on their sleds, her behind Ainsley and him behind Alec?

Or was it while they stood on the sidewalk of town square, the four of them, warming their hands with steamy cups of hot chocolate as they watched a parade of vehicles of all sorts and sizes decorated with colorful lights and Christmas-themed paraphernalia?

Or maybe it was the first time she looked into his eyes and saw the true man behind that silly scarf he wore because she truly believed that Colin Haney was a good man, just as Allie had said. A man who could be trusted to be loyal and loving. A man who deserved so much more than someone as flawed and damaged as she.

And what would she do with this newfound knowledge? Would she risk her heart, or more importantly, would she risk his?

These questions brought her thoughts back to a conversation she'd had with Hank the other day on her way to the bookstore.

"Why is it you're always here? In the park, I mean."

Hank gave her one of his usual sideways glances. "Probably for the same reason you're drawn here day after day. The fresh air. The open space. It all seems to makes thinking easier somehow, don't you agree?"

He's probably right about that, she'd thought to herself.

"And you know what I think about, Gracie, day after day after day? What the hell did I do with my life?"

Grace had given him that same sideways glance before she said, "I suppose we all have mistakes in our past, but some are worse than others."

"True. Doesn't mean they're irredeemable, though."

She'd turned to face him. "So, is that what you think about day after day after day? How to rectify those mistakes?"

He'd chuckled at that. "Believe me, I think of nothing else."

"So, it isn't too late, then?"

His mouth had twisted into a grin that didn't reach his eyes. "If you'd asked me that a couple of weeks ago, I'd have given you a different answer, but today, I think not. Today, I'm thinking I've still got a chance."

CHAPTER 27

"Grace?"

Spinning, she found Colin standing in the doorway wearing only the bottoms to the pajamas she had picked out for him, a myriad of questions, mixed with need and desire all shining in his eyes. Even from that distance, she felt the heat of his gaze as it scaled her form.

His mouth turned up at the corners. "I am so glad we agreed to choose each other's outfits for this impromptu getaway. That pink is definitely your color, and as for the rest... All I can say is *wow*."

Fidgeting with the thin strap of the ankle-length lingerie, she forced a smile. "I have to admit, you did so well with your choices that I had to wonder how much experience you've had." Colin raised a brow, prompting Grace to clarify. "I'm talking about picking out lingerie."

"Oh, well, this was my first, actually." She gave him a look, telling him that she doubted that statement, and he let out a bark of laughter. "I swear. No *serious* relationships before now, nothing more than—"

"Colin—"

"No, let me finish." Moving closer, one slow step at a time, he said, "I know you see this thing between us as only temporary. I get it. You're leaving in... What are we down to now, one week? Less?"

Her throat clogged with emotion making it hard to speak, so she did no more than nod in response.

"So, I get it," he went on. "I get that you've been living— No," he said with a shake of his head, "let me rephrase because I don't get that part at all. I don't understand why you won't allow yourself a *life*. Why you deny yourself the simplest of contacts, of connecting with the people who want and crave that connection with you.

"You're worth it, Grace. You're more than worthy of love, so why won't you give us a chance?"

"Colin, I..." Closing the last several feet of space between them, she splayed her hands on his bare chest and let out a sigh. "I've been doing that all day, all week even—giving it a chance, or trying to— but how fair is this to you? You imagine this *thing* between us, this connection as something more, and how fair is that? How can I even consider staying in St. Thaddaeus, staying with *you* when you don't know..."

Grasping her hands in his and holding them to his heart, he said, "It pains me to say this, but you're a liar, Grace St. John."

Shocked by his frankness, she could do no more than look up at him with her mouth hanging open.

"You haven't been trying, Grace, you've been pretending to, and there's a huge difference. So, I'm going to ask you for a favor. Give yourself and me this one night. No talk of the past and no thought of tomorrow. Just tonight and just us. No confessions, no fears, no worries. Just me. Just you. And just this."

He wrapped his arms around her and crushed her mouth with his releasing the sweet, sweet taste of passion, desire, and need, filling her from the core of her soul to every nerve ending.

Heat pooled in her center as his mouth moved over hers in a dance as old as time, as they explored and learned each other's taste, reveled in each other's touch, and celebrated the gasps of arousal.

Her breasts swelled with desire and a need to be touched, to be cherished, an ache she couldn't remember ever having felt before.

So she opened to him. Opened her mouth, opened her arms, and pulled him closer, taking him in just as he'd asked, with no more pretending that this wasn't what she wanted, what she craved just as much as he.

She would grant him that favor but just for tonight. For right now, she would give him her all, but not without the illusions still between them. For she knew that come tomorrow, the secret she held would tear them apart.

Colin slid an arm under her knees, lifted her, and carried her to the bed. He laid her down and stood above her, one knee on the mattress, one foot on the floor, pausing to take in every little thing about her.

The glow of her silky curls in the soft light of the fire coming from the other room.

Those sad yet beautiful green eyes, their silver specks reflecting heat and desire back at him.

That luscious giving mouth, the soft, luminescent skin...

He climbed onto the bed, but before he could lower himself to her completely, Grace turned to her side, hinting that she wanted him to lie next to her instead.

Now on his back with her propped on an elbow and leaning slightly over him, he said, "I don't want you to feel pressured, Grace. We don't have to—"

"I don't feel pressured," she responded, placing her fingers over his lips. "I don't, I promise. I want this just as much as you do, but you'll have to give me this concession. I can't... I can't have you over me."

Colin instantly shoved the images that request brought to the forefront of his mind. "Of course. You lead, Grace, and I'll be right here with you."

She nodded and bent to him, brushing her hand over his bicep, skimming his pecs and scrapping his abs with the tips of her nails.

Her touch caused him to shiver as he ached to give her the same thrill, but a promise was a promise, and he wouldn't risk breaking the spell.

Their lips met again, touching, tasting, savoring, and sinking in. She gasped into his mouth, allowing him to capture her breath, and the intensity doubled.

They undressed each other in a frenzy of need, yet with every fresh inch of skin he exposed, Colin knew he would remember these moments forever. The feel of her hands on his skin and his on hers. How passion deepened the green of her eyes and how her lips parted and her moans of pleasure caused him to stiffen with an ache so divine he thought his heart would burst.

But he wanted to savor, to explore and cherish. To show her what she could have if only she would let him in.

Overwhelmed. Everything about Colin, about this night had been overwhelming, but now, here, at this moment, Grace was so swamped with yearning, she could think of nothing else.

The need for Colin to hold her, to love her, and to never let go.

So, she would take what he offered if only for one night. If that's all this was, if that's all she could have, then she would take it and never forget.

Never forget how perfect, how wonderful, and how right it felt. And she would give. Give him that much and more, share with him everything she had inside her to spare.

She straddled his thighs as her lips grazed his chin and next his shoulder.

She reared up at the exquisite glide of his palms over her rib cage to encompass her hips and move on to her legs.

Those marvelous fingers skimmed her sensitive skin from her knees to the apex of her thighs. And when she rose again, he molded her breasts, circled their peaks, and never once allowed his gaze to lose its connection with hers.

She took him in, all of him, both of them sighing at the exquisite heat, the length of him deep inside her, filling her, stretching her, touching her in ways no one else ever had before or would again.

Then they began to move in another dance as old as time but this one more intimate, more precious.

More everything.

CHAPTER 28

Dinner had been delicious, Grace was sure, although she couldn't swear to it as she hadn't tasted a bite. And the Haneys couldn't have been nicer nor tried any harder to make her feel comfortable. The problem was, Grace couldn't remember ever being part of a family dinner; she didn't know how to do this.

And yet, the twins' non-stop chatter over the dinner table was exactly what she'd needed to keep to her from fleeing. Between their funny stories involving friends at school and a word for word recitation of this year's letters to Santa, there hadn't been a spare moment for Grace to remember how out of her comfort zone this evening truly was.

Colin lay on the floor at her feet, panting with near exhaustion after wrestling with the wild animals who looked strangely enough like miniature humans. After double helpings of creamy, sugary desserts, it was no wonder the twins were bouncing around the Haneys' great room as if they were Tigger's long-lost relatives.

Grace couldn't stop laughing, especially as she watched Alec sneak his fourth chocolate ball from a nearby candy dish.

Lizbeth and Duncan had insisted on cleaning up dinner, just the two of them, leaving Colin and Grace alone with the twins for the better part of an hour.

Lizbeth came into the room then, clapping her hands together and putting an immediate halt to the merriment going on around them. "Okay, you two. If that tree falls over on your heads, you're sleeping in the barn tonight with the rest of the animals, and I don't care how cold it is out there." "Can we?" Ainsley pleaded. "Please, Nana?"

With a shake of her head, Lizbeth looked down at Colin, who was trying his best not to show his amusement. "Son, why don't you go on and take Grace home while I give these two a good dunking in the tub with some bubbles?" Bursts of *'yippee"* rang in the air around them as Colin jumped to his feet. "By the time you get back," his mother continued, "I'll have them ready for bed and cozied up with the cows."

The twins broke out in more hysterical giggles, rolling on the floor.

"You have cows?" Grace asked.

"She's just kidding."

"Oh. Well, it isn't necessary for you to take me home. I can walk. I've been walking to and from the bookstore—"

"Nonsense," Duncan interrupted with a scoff as he came into the room, wiping his hands with a dishtowel.

Colin took hold of her hand. "Don't argue. I drove you here, I'll drive you home, and since we were running late this morning and I took you directly to the bookstore, I've still got your shopping bags in the car. Plus, it's probably no more than ten degrees outside. You're not walking, Grace."

She knew he would insist, but couldn't stop herself from holding out hope for a little more time. But the promise she made was only for one night, and she hadn't thought of anything else all day.

Grace nodded, and the craziness started up again with hoots, hollers, laughter, and a flurry of commotion.

The twins barreled into her, throwing their arms around her legs. "Ga'night," Alec whispered in her ear as she bent to his level, his chocolatey breath as sweet and endearing as his warm hug.

"Goodnight, Alec. Thank you for showing me your army men."

"They're not army," he explained, "and a couple of them are girls. They're more indy'pendants, a black ops team or what Uncle calls a para...a para..."

"Paramilitary organization," Colin finished for him.

"Yeah, that. They're special and only called to duty for the really hard stuff."

"Oh, I see. Well, let's hope I never need to call on them."

Ainsley crawled up Grace's leg, not relenting until she pulled the child into a hug. Such affection was foreign to Grace, and by the glances thrown her way, she imagined it showed.

"Don't forget to say your prayers before you go to bed," Ainsley instructed with a serious face. "And 'member, you promised to sit with us in church again. I'll leave room so you can sit by me."

"I remember." After another bear hug and kiss on the cheek that didn't feel quite as awkward as it had less than a minute ago with Alec, Grace put Ainsley down and patted her on the head, a sudden rush of emotion making it hard for her to look anyone in the eye.

These kids were getting way too attached, and so was she. Christmas was only days away, and then she'd be gone, on her way to a new town, a new job, and her usual half-existence.

Gathering her wits, Grace pushed those thoughts away and turned to her hosts, bidding them goodnight as Colin ushered her out and into the night, along with a fresh wave of panic.

She had known better than to let it go this far and as wonderful and intoxicating as yesterday and last night had been, she had known it was all nothing more than a fantasy and one that soon would come to an end.

****

With a sideways glance, Colin studied Grace's features. "Hey. You okay over there?"

She nodded but didn't avert her gaze from the passing scenery even though it was too dark to see farther than the edge of the road. "Sure. Why wouldn't I be?"

"You tell me. You've barely said a word in the past five minutes."

"Just thinking, I guess."

"I gathered as much and, to be honest, that's what has me concerned. I have to admit, I fully expected you to try to worm your way out of tonight altogether. I even had my rebuttal prepared just in case."

She laughed, but Colin couldn't find even a hint of humor in its sweet sound. "I thought about it."

"I knew you would."

This time her laughter was genuine, and with a quick glance, Colin could see the amusement in her eyes.

"So, tell me this argument. I'd like to hear it."

"Well," he began, settling into one of their always easy conversations, "I've forgotten the exact words I'd prepared, but I would have started by telling you about the hours my mother spent on the menu and slaving over a hot stove just to make sure everything was perfect. And how Pop couldn't wait to tell you those embellished stories about my excellent grades or my very short baseball career that went no further than high school."

"And if neither of those tactics had worked?"

"Then I would have gone in for the kill by using the twins. You're so good with them, Grace, and they never stop asking when they're going to see you again."

Several beats passed before a heartbreaking sob filled the taut silence. Colin immediately pulled over to the side of the otherwise deserted road.

They were on the outskirts of town where the road bordered an edge of Angel Tree Farms. The side that harvested several species of oaks, with line upon line of deciduous trees, their branches resembled twisted arms and gnarled fingers reaching for the heavens above and begging for another season, another chance at life.

Colin put his vehicle in park and turned to face her.

Beyond that one sob, Grace held it all inside, but he could see the struggle. It was clear in her eyes, written on her face, and evident in the trembling of the hands covering her mouth.

He released her seatbelt as he did his own and pulled her into his embrace without saying a word. Nothing needed to be said—not by him.

They had made love all through the night and again this morning, both knowing that their intimate cocoon was only temporary. Knowing that they would come back to reality and with that, both memories of the past and fears of the future would come crashing back upon them.

He had hoped to hold it all off for a little longer. But right here, right now, he only needed to hold her, to assure her that she was safe. Safe from the pain and hurt he could only imagine she had suffered in the past. Safe from the loneliness and isolation that filled her life until now. And he could only pray to the Lord above that she would let him in, allow him to erase that pain, wipe the hurt from her memory, and make the self-induced isolation and loneliness a thing of her past.

She stiffened at his touch, but he held on—not tightly, nor confining as he'd learned last night brought her intense fear—only close enough, firm enough to let her be the one to decide.

Seconds later, she wrapped her arms around him and clung. When he finally felt her body soften and heard her breathing regulate, he eased back, brushed a lock of honey-blonde hair from her brow, and waited for the silent tears to abate.

"Talk to me, Grace. I can sense that you want to, and I need you to know you can."

It took her a few tries to get the words out, but eventually, she did. "I don't want to hurt you. I don't want to hurt *them*. Alec and Ainsley don't deserve that."

"Why would you hurt those kids? How would you?"

"Because I'll leave just like their parents did. I'm not saying this because I don't care about them but because I *do*. You can't allow them to get attached, Colin. You have to put a stop to it. Now."

"No. No, I won't. *You're* the one who has to stop this, Grace. Stop pushing everyone away, stop pushing *me* away."

With a vehement shake of her head, she argued, "You don't understand—"

"Then help me to understand. Talk to me."

Instead of a reply, her lips thinned, and that almost stubborn jaw clenched. Colin huffed a sigh, mumbling under his breath about stubborn women and foolish souls.

He pulled one knee up onto the front seat, folded his arms over his chest, and settled in. "I'd hoped that last night showed you how I felt about you. That no matter what happened in your past, that's all it is, Grace, nothing but your *past*. Whatever it is, it only defines you if you let it. It only dictates your future if you allow it to. It only keeps me from loving you if you keep pushing me away."

Grace sat there, still and silent as Colin took a deep, bracing breath and went on. "Tell me something. How do you see your future once you leave St. Thaddaeus? Where will you go, Grace? Will you go on as you have for, I don't know how many years? Will you go back to living a life that's no life at all? Do you have no hopes, no dreams for something more?"

"Foster kids don't have the luxury of dreams!" she shouted, chocking on another sob. "There's no room for them. There's only room for surviving that day and the next."

Colin winced. "I hate that you had to go through that, Grace. I despise knowing that you didn't have the love and protection that you needed, that you deserved when you were a child, but don't you understand that the only person preventing you from having that now is *you*?"

"You're right. It is me. But what you don't understand is that I've tried being normal, I tried living like everyone else, and I failed. I failed because... Because..."

He took her hand in his and gave it a light squeeze. "I'm not trying to make you go anywhere it's too painful to go," he said, deliberately softening his tone, "but help me to understand what you're afraid of. If you talk about what happened to you, if you open up, maybe it will help you to let it go."

She closed her eyes, but only for a moment, then straightened her shoulders and lifted her chin. "You want me to tell you about the emotional and physical abuse, Colin? About the neglect and the years of living in-between. In-between homes, in-between families. In-between *everything*? Never a part of something, never belonging anywhere or to anyone?

"You want to hear about the sexual abuse, Colin, about what—" Her voice faltered, so she started again. "You imagine that I'll tell you I was raped, and that's why I panicked that day in my kitchen, why I couldn't stand the thought of you on top of me. But you'd be wrong. I wasn't raped, Colin. Nearly but not, not like the others as I laid there and did nothing to stop him. While I said nothing and told no one what was going on."

Stopping her, he said, "Tell me about these charges Chief Daniels spoke about." Grace jolted with a note of surprise. As if she didn't expect him to go there. But watching her, seeing the pain those memories brought in her eyes, prompted him to steer the conversation in a slightly different direction. "The police chief wouldn't tell me what the charges were, but he did say they'd been dropped. Does that have anything to do with why you say you tried and failed at being normal?"

Grace stared out into the dark. The only light in the vehicle came from the dashboard, the only sound their breathing and the soft whir of the artificial heat keeping them warm.

Colin remained silent, giving her as much time as she needed, and after a long, intense minute, she began. "The moment you turn eighteen, you're no longer part of the foster care system, you're on your own. I was lucky in that I had Father Tim because he'd helped me to get ready for that day. I had a decent paying job, and an apartment already lined up. Father Tim vouched for me for the job and co-signed on the apartment. He knew I wouldn't let him down."

She glanced Colin's way, and he nodded, letting her know he was listening, that he cared, and that he was right there.

"The job was stocking shelves at this bookstore in the local mall. I always liked to read; Father taught me that I could live in another world in books, worlds where I didn't have to be alone, so I lived in those worlds more often than the real one.

"Anyway, things were going pretty well, I had a job and a few friends, and just after my nineteenth birthday, I met Roger. We started dating, and it quickly turned into this *thing*. We saw each other nearly every day, and before I knew it, he was at my apartment all the time.

"About three months into the relationship, I gave him a key. I trusted him. I believed he meant it when he said he loved me. I told him things about my past that I hadn't talked about with anyone other than Father Tim. I'd let him in, and not just in my apartment and in my bed."

She stopped then and looked Colin in the eyes, the expression on her face indicating that she was waiting to be judged. But Colin said nothing. Again, he didn't interrupt, only waited in silence, giving her time to choose how much more she would say. Time to choose if she would trust again because clearly, her trust in Roger had been a mistake.

After another long pause, she resumed her tale. "I preface my story with all that information to show you that Roger *knew*. He *knew*, and he preyed on my fears. Matter-of-fact, I found out later that he had planned it all out like some twisted joke he'd arranged with his buddies."

"Planned what, exactly?" Colin asked, leaning forward and taking her hand in his, hoping his touch would give her the courage to go on.

"This one night I had to work until closing and Roger had gone out with friends. I remember being so tired when I got home that I nearly went to bed without even changing my clothes. I think I fell asleep within seconds. But...sometime later, I was awakened by this suffocating weight on top of me. It was dark, and I had been dead asleep, I didn't—"

She shook her head, swallowed and swallowed again, blinking back tears and taking deep breaths. "When the police came Roger said I'd attacked him and I couldn't deny it because I had. I used the knife that I kept under my pillow. But he knew, Colin. Roger *knew* I kept it there.

"Still, he–he acted as though he was dumbfounded that I would react like that. The blade had grazed his arm in our struggles, and Roger was furious that I'd actually drawn blood. He started ranting about it no longer being a joke, and he called the police. He insisted they arrest me for assault. Since he had a key to my apartment and a neighbor who swore he'd been living there with me for the past few months, the police officers said they couldn't charge Roger with unlawful entry or trespassing, and since there were no marks on me and I wouldn't say that he'd done anything wrong, they had no choice but to go with his side of the story."

Struggling to keep his breathing even, to hold his anger inside, Colin asked only one question. "Which was what?"

"Roger said he'd been out at the bar with his buddies, and I was angry that he'd come home drunk. That I'd attacked him after accusing him of being with another girl."

Colin closed his eyes and prayed for strength. The strength to hold his temper because he wanted nothing more than to find this asshole and wring his fat neck.

"How did it come about that the charges were dropped?"

"Father Tim. Once again, he came to my rescue. I don't know the whole of it, all I know is that Father sat Roger down and convinced him to tell the truth; that he'd purposely meant to scare me. The police also confirmed that Roger wasn't on the lease, that it was my apartment, and mine alone. I imagine that, and a few other things are what convinced the DA to drop the charges."

Colin nodded. "So that's what Chief Daniels meant when he said you weren't trying to protect yourself from getting hurt but that you were trying to protect *me*. Which is ridiculous, Grace. First, because I'm no Roger and I would never do something like that, and second, just because that happened once doesn't mean it would happen again."

"No, Colin. That wasn't the first time, and I have every intention of it being the last."

CHAPTER 29

After discarding their heavy winter coats and gloves, and dropping her bags on the sofa, Grace headed for the kitchen to put on a pot of water for tea with Colin following close on her heels.

She filled the tea kettle and set it on the stove to boil, but before she could flick on the burner, he took hold of her shoulders and turned her to face him.

He held her steady by wrapping his palms around her upper arms. "Look. I don't want you to think I asked you to wait to tell me anything more because I don't want to hear it. That's not why I suggested we finish this conversation here."

"Then, why did you?"

"Because I needed a few minutes, and *not* for the reason you're imagining," he added when Grace opened her mouth to speak. "I just needed a little time to go from wanting to murder Roger to only wanting to smash his face in."

Grace looked momentarily surprised, but within a matter of seconds, a bubble of what sounded like nervous laughter rose up and spilled out between her lips. "And have you had enough time to calm down, G.I. Joe?"

"'G.I. Joe?'"

Grace lifted her shoulders. "He's the first macho character who came to mind, which could possibly have something to do with Alec's paramilitary black ops team."

As Colin followed Grace's tentative grin from her mouth to her eyes, he watched the false amusement fade and felt her shiver from deep within.

"I also wanted to give *you* a moment to be sure," he said.

"Sure?"

"I don't want you to feel as if you *need* to tell me like you're obligated to. I promised I would never step over the line with you, Grace, and I meant it. What I'm trying to say is, I want to know that I've earned your trust before you give it."

A soft sigh from between her parted lips preceded the brush of her hand on his cheek. Colin captured that hand before she had a chance to pull away and pressed his lips into her palm.

She shook her head. "I *need* to tell you—not out of obligation but out of respect. And not only respect for you but for your parents, Allie, Charlie, and everyone else in this town. More importantly, because those children need you and I can't risk it happening again. I won't put *you* at risk, Colin, and I never should have allowed things to go so far without telling you all this beforehand."

"You did nothing wrong by keeping your secrets to yourself, Grace. And as for the other, it *won't* happen again. You didn't plan to hurt that bastard—"

"Colin, stop and listen to me!" she cried, breaking away from his hold and stepping back. "Listen to what I'm trying to tell you because you're not hearing me."

Her breathing was more erratic now, coming out in harsh pants, but it wasn't passion that had her blood pumping. Her eyes were wide and wild, and her hands were visibly shaking. Colin wanted desperately to hold her again, but he knew the best he could do for her now was to stay right where he was.

"I *did* plan it," she spit out as her teeth began to chatter. "I kept that knife under my pillow, and I had every intention of using it."

"Grace—"

"I *told you it wasn't the first time!*" Silent tears streamed down her face, but she appeared calmer somehow, perhaps resigned to how she expected this to end. She took a step closer again, her hands out in front of her as if begging him to listen, then a moment later, her face crumpled.

"Before Roger... Years before that...I killed someone. He... He was only a boy, just fourteen, and I killed him. I killed him."

CHAPTER 30

So far, Saturday had gone by in a blur. Having cried herself to sleep the night before, Grace woke with her eyes swollen and her face puffy.

As her dinner break rolled around, she was too exhausted to eat, so instead, she made her way to the storage room where she curled up in a corner and attempted to shut down.

But no matter how hard she tried, scenes from last night, the night before that, and all the days preceding since she'd stumbled upon this town continued to bounce around in her head, simply refusing to settle.

She hadn't seen nor heard from Colin since he left her last night, after assuring her that they would talk again today and finish their discussion.

He had kissed her deeply, passionately, and said he hadn't wanted to leave her, but his parents were waiting, and so he had to go. But something had warned her—whether real or imagined—that last night's kiss might very well be their last.

Still, she'd half expected him to show up at some point today— her lunch break, at least, as he had every day these past weeks—but he never did.

Of course, she had insisted Allie take her lunch break first and then begged the co-worker to bring her back a sandwich, so she didn't have to risk finding Colin waiting for her at Pat's.

Naturally, Allie argued the point having seen right through her, which only served to force Grace to play the "Didn't you say you'd always have my back" card. It worked, too, although grudgingly, and Grace eventually got her way even though missing Colin as she did only made the long afternoon even harder.

The twins were a no-show for storytime that afternoon as well, which hurt Grace more than she could have imagined. But then, hadn't she insisted that he keep them away?

She pressed her fingers to her lips and fought back the tears as the memory of their one intimate night together replayed in her mind.

Colin wasn't her first as he knew, but never had it been like that. Never could she remember feeling so safe, so wanted, so cherished. And never had she wanted so much more.

Over this last week, in particular, the revelations had racked up, one after another. The most prominent at this moment was that as hard as she had tried to remain outside looking in, this town and these people had pulled her inside regardless. And for the first time in memory, she wanted desperately to find her way.

She wanted a chance at the kind of future Allie had put in her head. A future with friends who stayed true and didn't falter. A future with neighbors who didn't skulk around in the night looking for ways to hurt one another, and a community that went deeper than simply working and living side by side, but with people who truly cared, who protected and nurtured one another without an ulterior motive.

A future with someone special at her side; someone who genuinely cared about her, loved her and didn't betray that love by throwing it away.

By throwing *her* away.

But she had no idea how to go about gaining any of those things. How do you ask for something you know very well you don't deserve?

You don't, she told herself. She couldn't. But she could make a change.

The citizens of St. Thaddaeus and the Haneys, especially, had shown her that good people did exist and that somewhere, someday, she just might feel as though she'd found where she belonged.

Then another revelation struck, and Grace knew what she had to do—what her first step toward her new future would have to be.

She had to begin by saying goodbye.

Moving to Charlie's desk, she pulled her cell phone from her pocket, and with her heart racing, her lungs near to seizing, she once again pulled up that familiar number.

As the ringing began, Grace held her breath, wrapping her fingers around the phone so tightly she feared the device might crack. After four long rings, the call finally connected, and once again, voicemail answered.

She paid little attention to the words this time, waiting for the message to end.

"...I'm sorry I wasn't here to take your call, but please leave a message, and I promise to get back to you as soon as I can."

For the first time in a very long while, Grace stayed on the line, and after the beep, she swallowed hard, then began to speak.

"I love you. I love you so very, very much, and I never truly thanked you for loving me back. I never truly thanked you for always being there and for never giving up on me. For all the years you tried knocking some sense into this hard head and for showing me the way. I'm so sorry I didn't listen. And I'm so very sorry that I never told you how much you meant to me."

After Grace disconnected the call, she made another. This one required following a list of instructions such as press two for this and six for that; enter your account number and the last four digits of your social. Finally, she reached an actual person.

"How can I help today?" the pleasant voice on the other end asked.

"Yes, I need to have this telephone number canceled, please."

"That's fine. I see that you've been off contract for some time. Is there anything we can do to continue serving you?"

"No. There's no purpose... Just close the account, please, and there's no reason to wait until the end of the billing cycle. Just disconnect the line immediately."

"Yes, ma'am. I'll take care of it right away."

"Thank you." She hung up, closed her eyes, and gathering what little reserve she had left for step two, Grace pulled a pen and sheet of paper from Charlie's desk drawer.

Father Tim:

As promised, I haven't stopped attending Mass, and yes, Father Stephen seems like a good man; he's kind and patient, and like you, always ready with an ear. But even still, I can't confess to him my sins for fear of being judged, fear of being turned away, of being deemed unworthy of forgiveness and redemption.

Father, I need you. I need you to convince me that there's a purpose for me here, some reason you saved me and kept me under your wing because I'm finding it harder and harder to believe.

Where are those witty words of wisdom you so often imparted when I need them most? The unfailing encouragement and the constant lectures about allowing the hand of God to guide me?

You promised you would always be here for me, but you're not and haven't been for such a long time. You said if I listened, if I had faith, I could always hear you, but I no longer do. I can't because with each passing day since you left me, month by month, and year by year, your voice fades a little more.

You left me alone with no way to reach you other than these letters, and this one-way correspondence is no longer hitting its mark.

Why? Why did you leave me here all alone? And didn't God know I needed you more?

Forever Missing You,
Grace

CHAPTER 31

Drained of all emotion since her dinner break, Grace worked the remainder of her Saturday shift on auto-pilot. She painted on a smile, thanked every customer, and wished them all a "Merry Christmas." She assisted in searches for the perfect gift or the perfect card, straightened shelves, and tidied supplies.

Other than the expected books, magazines, and newspapers, Charlie carried notecards of all sizes, and greeting cards for all occasions, all kinds of stationery, calendars, diaries, and journals, and any writing supplies you could possibly need. Not to mention, games, puzzles, and a whole lot more. That meant there was always plenty to be done, and with this being the last weekend before Christmas, only a few days left, in fact, business at the bookstore continued to bustle all the way up until closing.

With mere minutes to go, Grace was in the rear of the store, straightening a stack of colored pencils when she heard the jingle of the bell over the front door.

Her head lifted, and she held her breath.

If it was Colin, what would she say?

Would she be able to stop herself from running into his arms and begging for a chance at redemption?

Several more seconds ticked by then came Charlie's happy exclamation, "That's the last customer for tonight. Time to go home, Grace."

Her eyes closed for a brief moment and released the breath she'd been holding, just as Charlie appeared from behind a tall shelf. Plastering on a forced smile, she turned to face him. "Finally. I thought this day would never end, and I'm beat."

Charlie tilted his head with a look of concern in his eyes that Grace no longer doubted was true. "You do look tired, I'm sorry to say. There's nothing wrong, though, I hope?"

"I'm good," Grace replied, avoiding eye contact. But as she started to turn and head for the storeroom for her coat and gloves, she hesitated and turned back. "Charlie. I want you to know that I've enjoyed working here. You and Allie, especially, have been... Well, you've been friends like none I've ever known, and I'll never forget that."

Her words prompted another head tilt, but Charlie seemed to understand she wasn't going to offer more. He cleared his throat. "Well, speaking for myself, I'm more pleased than you could know that you found us. And Grace... If you change your mind about staying on, you've got a place here at the bookstore. You know that, right?"

"I appreciate that, but—"

"No, don't say anything just now. You go on home and get a good night's sleep. I promise you everything will be clearer in the morning. Did you drive in today, Grace, or walk?"

"I drove," she lied again, knowing that if Charlie knew she planned to walk home, he would insist on giving her a lift.

"All right, then," he said with a satisfied nod. "You head on out while I lock up. Sleep in and make the most of your Sunday."

"I'll try. Goodnight, Charlie."

"Night, Grace."

After slipping on her winter wear, she headed out, considering only briefly stopping by Pat's to order some take out. Pat had become a dear friend, even though Grace hadn't admitted that before, not to him or herself. But she didn't think she could possibly handle seeing him just now without falling apart.

She stood just outside the store, taking a long moment to inhale a gulp of the crisp, cold night air, along with the rest of the atmosphere. The sidewalks were nearly deserted this late at night, the lights in the store windows reflecting a rainbow of colors onto the wet pavement. The holiday decorations hanging from the street lamps glittered against the glow of the moon, and the town Christmas tree that stood tall in the center of the square gleamed with white lights and colored balls.

It was peaceful and quiet, yet bright and alive at the same time; all of it so full of hope and happiness and joy.

Grace felt none of that.

Recalling that she had told Charlie a fib, two actually, she pushed forward and started toward the park at a brisk pace, making it no more than ten feet before coming to an abrupt halt.

From the corner of her eye, she could swear she'd just seen a figure standing before the Christmas tree, someone looking up and...

Was that a pair of angel's wings protruding...

With a shake of her hear, Grace looked again and saw a blur of white.

Prompted to act without further hesitation, she crossed the road with hurried steps, bouncing up onto the sidewalk on the opposite side on the balls of her feet, each step two times her usual gait.

As she approached the exact spot where the figure had stood only moments before, Grace slowed just long enough to glance over at the angel statute with suspicion, then around the Christmas tree she went, coming to a stop as she nearly collided with someone hiding in the dark.

"Goodness gracious me!" Mary Francis exclaimed with a hand to her heart. "Grace St. John, you nearly startled the black clean off my hide. Right about now, I must be near as white as you are."

Grace squinted into the glare of the Christmas lights. "It's Mary Francis, isn't it?" The woman nodded, her grin wide. "What are you doing out here at this time of night?"

Mary Francis waved a dismissive hand in the air. "Oh, I was just havin' a word with the good Lord, is all. Or I suppose you could say he was havin' a word with me. You wouldn't happen to be walking home now, would you?"

Grace straightened with uncertainty. "Why do you ask?"

"Well, I was about to head on home myself, you see, and not that I'm scared, mind you, but I wouldn't say no to a little company."

"Oh, of course. Which way—"

"I enjoy cutting through Araqiel Park," Mary Francis interrupted, slipping her arm through Grace's, "and I hear you do too. 'Course, I'm on the east side of town and not as far out as you are, but if we stick together at least until reachin' Raphael Path, I'd be more'an grateful."

With a nod, Grace stuck her free hand in her pocket, wrapped her fingers around the envelope inside, and struck out at a slower pace with Mary Francis at her side.

They walked in silence for the first little while, each seemingly deep in their own thoughts until they reached the park where silver bells hung from the trees and bright red bows adorned the old-fashioned street lamps that lit the paths, mimicking the decorations of town square, although to a much lesser degree.

There were a few other St. Thad citizens out and about, but everyone seemed so far away that it gave the illusion of being completely alone.

Reminding Grace that she *wasn't* alone, Mary Francis said, "It's a shame you havin' to leave so soon an' all. I thought for sure you'd stay at least until after the new year."

Grace shot her a look. "Charlie only needed an extra employee through Christmas. Allie said herself that—"

"Oh, don't give me that?" Mary Francis exclaimed, stopping short. "Are you goin' to tell me Charlie hasn't asked you to stay on?"

"Well, no," Grace mumbled, ashamed of herself for attempting to tell another fib. "He never came right out and asked, and although he made it clear that I *could* stay on if I wanted to, I'm pretty sure he only said that because he felt he had to."

Mary Francis *tsk*ed and shook her head. "I imagine you know better than to tell such lies, Grace St. John, but I'll let you go on that one, seeing as it's an itty-bitty one. Now, Colin Haney, he's a good'un. A real decent man who helps his momma and poppa, takes such good care of those poor babies—who could really use a mamma of their own if you don't mind me sayin' so—and that man *never, ever* tells a lie without some good reason behind it."

Grace frowned but didn't comment.

"Oh, he may tease up a storm," Mary Francis went on, "Colin's got hisself one doozy of a sense of humor, don't he? But he never means any harm. Which is why it near tore me to pieces seeing him so broken-hearted last night."

"Last night?"

"Yes'um. I saw him right after he done took you home. He wanted to turn his car around, but he's a responsible one, he is, so he hurried on back to get those babies home to bed. I ran into his mamma today too and asked her how he was doin', and you know what she said?"

Grace shook her head.

"She told me that her boy was just a sorry sort today. That he was a short-tempered grouch and all kinds of sad. She said he was a pinin' bad for someone if you can believe it, and I thought to myself, why, whoever that girl is, she must not know what she's got right under her nose if that boy has to pine away in misery."

"Maybe he woke up with a clear head this morning."

"Oh? And why do you think so, if you don't mind me askin'?"

Grace wasn't about to get into her confessions of last night, so instead, she shrugged. "I haven't heard from him all day. That kind of says it all, I think."

Mary Francis *tsk*ed again before lapsing into an awkward silence.

With a sideways glance, Grace began, "You said earlier that you were having a conversation with God—"

The woman laughed. "Well, I wouldn't say we was conversating, exactly. Lord knows he don't always talk back."

"Doesn't that get...? Don't you ever feel like...why bother?"

"Lordy, no. Just 'cause I don't hear His words doesn't mean I don't feel 'em. Just look around you, Grace. Look around and see with your heart and soul. Heed God's signs, and He will lead you home."

Having reached the start of the eastern pathway where they would part, Mary Francis waved a hand over its marker. "All you gots to do is follow the right path," she said.

And for the umpteenth time in the past twenty-four hours, tears welled in Grace's eyes. Blinking them back, she bid Mary Francis a goodnight then turned to make her way.

However, before taking even one step in that direction, Grace realized there was no reason why she shouldn't see Mary Francis all the way to her destination. So, she twisted around, intent on calling out to the woman, only to stop short as Mary Francis was no longer in sight. The eastern path leading out of the park and into the neighborhood beyond was empty.

Grace stood there a minute longer, wondering if the woman had merely veered from the path or if she was just lighter and quicker on her feet than Grace had imagined.

With a shrug, she started toward home, but then remembered that she hadn't ventured this way before, and this path marker was one she hadn't yet seen. So, stepping into the light of the lamp above, she looked down and read:

Here you enter the path of Raphael,
Ruling angel of the east.
Allow these stepping stones to heal you,
Body, mind, and soul.
Listen for the information and guidance
carried in the breeze.
But most of all repair that which is broken,
And you will finally be at ease.

CHAPTER 32

Grace arrived well before the start of Mass with what she thought was a pretty decent plan. She would deliver her final letter before she could change her mind, then slip out the side door before the early morning parishioners began filing in.

However, ten minutes into her meeting with Father Stephen as the two of them sat in a front pew speaking in hushed voices, Grace ended up saying much more than she initially intended.

Taking her hands and clasping them between his, the Father said, "I'm humbled to have heard your confession this morning, Grace. That you would trust me with those secrets tells me I was right to transfer here to St. Thaddaeus. But your reluctance to talk to me sooner about this, prompts me to remind you that I'm not here to judge, only to listen and help you to heal."

"I know," she said, her head bowed. "I think what I've been most afraid of is that you would offer me forgiveness even though I don't deserve it."

"Oh? And why would you believe such a thing? Why would an eight-year-old child not deserve forgiveness for protecting herself the only way she could think to, as well as protecting the other children around her? For taking matters into her own hands when she believed she had no other recourse? It's the adults who were charged with protecting you who should be having such doubts, not you."

When Grace didn't reply, he went on. "I didn't know your Father Timothy, but with absolute confidence, I tell you that he didn't stand up for you simply because he cared for you or because he had positioned himself as your champion. He did so because he *knew* you deserved no less.

"So, you see, Grace, you seek redemption for something that needs no forgiveness, and at the same time, you refuse to accept it. But the real problem here, and I'm sorry to say this, but the only person holding that forgiveness back is *you*."

"Believe it or not, I think I'm beginning to understand that," she said, forcing a smile, "and I appreciate you pointing out my stubbornness in getting to this point."

"Not stubborn, Grace. Just a lost lamb who's still in need of a shepherd to guide her and help her find her way. And as for these letters of yours," he added referring directly to the one now tucked in the deep pocket of his cassock, "I have to wonder why it is you think you should stop writing them, or for that matter, why you continue to say you don't know if you believe."

"What do you mean?"

"Well, just think about it. You told me yourself that these letters are your way of keeping Father Timothy with you. A way to hold him in your heart and never stop hearing his words no matter how far away he might be."

Grace nodded in agreement.

"And have they done that for you," he asked.

Yes, but—"

"No, no, stop right there," he said, waving a hand in the air. "That answers my question well enough and also begs another. You also say you don't know if you believe in God, and yet you appear to believe, without question, that Father Timothy is in His keeping. Isn't that right?"

Grace tilted her head. "I guess—"

"So, you see, Grace, these letters of yours are no different than me saying a prayer to God. I may not hear His words in my ear or even in my head, for that matter. But that doesn't mean I don't feel them in my heart or stop allowing my faith in Him to feed my soul."

He patted her hand again before letting her go. "Now, you give all of that some thought, and I'll finish getting ready for—"

The doors swung open, and several parishioners hurried inside, shaking off the damp winter air. "Oh!" Father Stephen exclaimed, jumping to his feet. "It must be later than I thought. Excuse me."

As the priest rushed off, Grace rose, and ducking her head, she started for the front doors with a determined stride.

****

On the other side, Colin reached for the handle, pulled the door open wide, and sucked in a surprised breath as he came face to face with Grace. Relief followed, along with a craving he couldn't get enough of.

"Now I know why I couldn't find you this morning."

"Find me?" Grace squeaked.

"Yeah, I went by your place so we could talk in private, and I could get—" It dawned on him then that she had been heading out as they were coming in. "Where were you going?"

"I... I was—"

"Wait. Hold that thought." With a hand on Grace's arm, Colin maneuvered her back a step, allowing Ainsley and Alec to slide inside from under his arm while Duncan and Lizbeth came up the steps behind them.

Without giving Grace a chance to finish her sentence, he then entwined his fingers with hers and pulled her back down the aisle to slip into their customary pew.

As they removed their coats and settled in their seats, Colin looked over at Grace, who appeared more uncomfortable than he had ever seen her. There was so much he wanted to say, but now was not the time, and this was most definitely not the place, so, unfortunately, it would have to wait.

Ainsley climbed into Colin's lap. 'It's my turn to sit next to Grace, you promised, 'member?"

Of course, just—"

"Nuh-uh," Alec whined, "she got to sit next to Grace last time. It's my turn now."

Keeping his sigh internal, Colin brushed a hand across Alec's brow. "You both can, buddy. Squeeze in."

Once in their preferred places, both children looked up at Grace with a beatific grin and took one of her hands in theirs. Grace looked over at Colin with a pained expression.

He leaned in and whispered, "Don't worry, he isn't contagious; it was nothing more than too many sweets, too much activity, and not enough sleep. He's feeling much better as of this morning and insisted on coming to church for fear he'd have to wait another two whole days before he got to see you."

"See *me*?" Her brow crinkled as she looked down at Alec then back to Colin. "What are you talking about?"

Studying her face, he tilted his head. Was it possible she didn't know? That no one told her? "Alec kept me hopping—"

"I frowed up five times!" Alec proudly exclaimed.

Snickers and giggles came from the row behind them.

"You did?" Grace hugged Alec to her side.

"He frowed up all over the couch," Ainsley informed her, "and Pop had to bringed us a special vacuum from the store."

"Steam cleaner," Colin clarified.

"Yeah, and yesterday he frowed up in Uncle's bed, too, and Uncle had to wash the sheets three times!"

"Shh." Colin gave Ainsley one of those looks, who then snuggled into Grace's side with a wide grin.

Alec looked up at Grace, batted his baby blues, and stuck out his bottom lip. "I didn't mean to stink up the whole house."

"Oh, you poor baby," she said, hugging him closer.

Colin snorted. "Needless to say, I've ordered a new mattress and since the sofa was also out—"

"He had to sleep in my bed," Ainsley announced to the entire congregation, and more laughter erupted around them.

"Yeah, well, it was either that or the floor, and I can tell you that after getting kicked in the head several times, the floor's looking pretty good for tonight."

The church was quickly filling up, and Mass was about to start. Not wanting to set a bad example, Colin gave Grace's hand a reassuring squeeze and whispered, "We'll talk after."

CHAPTER 33

Grace didn't know which emotion of the dozen or so rushing through her was the most prominent or the most appropriate just now, but dread appeared to be spiking its way to the top of the pile as she and the others inched toward the exit of the church.

Father Stephen held his usual post at the doors, shaking hands and wishing his flock well, while Duncan and Lizbeth led their small pack, Colin took up the rear making sure the twins didn't get lost in the shuffle, and Grace was somewhere in the middle, one hand clasped in Alec's and the other in Ainsley's. Grace wasn't sure whether to bolt the second she broke out into fresh air or if finding a secluded spot where she and Colin could get this incredibly uncomfortable scene over with was the better choice.

As the frigid cold air finally struck her face a few minutes later, and Grace's foot hit the first concrete step, Colin came up behind her. She noted the quick shared look that was exchanged between him and his parents before Duncan and Lizbeth each took a child by the hand and pulled them down the steps. At the same time, Colin put a hand to Grace's back and guided her to the side where the large stone building blocked a bit of the biting wind.

"Grace. I don't like the look I've been seeing on your face for the past hour. I hated leaving you like that after the discussion we had the other night, but you know it couldn't be helped."

She nodded, not knowing what to say, and when he brushed a hand down her arm, she instantly stiffened.

Colin frowned. "I want you to stay right here while I go talk to Mom and Pop. I'm going to ask them to take the twins home with them for a bit so you and I can talk."

"There's no need—"

"The hell there isn't," he said with a bite to his tone. "I can tell just by looking at you that I don't like what's going through your head."

He sighed. "It's obvious you weren't aware that Alec was sick all day yesterday, last night, and the night before. I'm sorry for that. I just assumed you would have heard when you stopped by the hardware store."

"Why would I have gone to the hardware store," she asked, unable to hold back any longer, "and for that matter, why didn't you just call?"

Colin cupped her cheeks and forced her to look at him. "*I left my phone at your place,*" he explained putting an emphasis on each word "I thought when you discovered it, and I didn't make it out to you to pick it up, you would swing by the hardware store with it when you had a chance, and that's when you'd find out I was home with Alec. I also knew you were working a long shift yesterday, so when you didn't come by the house, I stupidly didn't think anything of it other than you were either too tired or worried about getting sick yourself."

Grace's hand flew to her mouth. She hated crying, especially in front of people, but the hot tears began rolling down her cheeks before she could stop them.

Colin put his arms around her and pulled her in close, whispering into her ear, "I'm sorry. I'm so sorry if you misunderstood."

Wrapping her arms around his waist, she burrowed into the secure comfort of his shoulder. "I thought I'd finally convinced you..."

He pulled back and lifted her face to his. "Convinced me to give up on you?"

She nodded.

"Never. *You* were the victim, Grace, and maybe that boy had been a victim long before then, which is how he went so wrong. Who knows? What I do know is that the eight-year-old you did nothing wrong. You didn't mean to take a life, you were only trying to save one."

"I only wanted it to stop!" she cried.

"Shh, I know, I know," he said, pulling her in again and hugging her close. "And I know you can never forget, Grace, I'm not even going to suggest you do, but it's long past time to forgive. It's long past time you gave yourself permission to live rather than just exist. Because we want you in our lives, Grace. I want you in my life, and I'll never stop trying to convince you that this is where you belong."

Releasing her, Colin brushed the drying tears from her cheeks with the pads of his thumbs. "So, what do you say? Will you stay? Will you give me and the rest of the family a chance to prove to you that here with me, with *us,* is where you belong?"

"I... I want to, but—"

Colin smiled and crushed his mouth to hers. But before Grace had a chance to truly sink into his kiss, someone cleared their throat.

Breaking the kiss, Colin turned, at the same time pulling Grace protectively into his side.

"Hey there, Zophiel," Colin said, greeting their intruder with a stiff nod.

Grace blinked in confusion. "What did you just call him?"

Colin chuckled. "Zophiel. Zee is just a nickname. Do you have a problem with this, Mayor?" Colin asked, tucking Grace just that much more into his embrace. "Because I'm pretty sure Miss St. John was just about to consent to stay on past Christmas."

For the first time ever, Zee looked directly at Grace with something other than a scowl on his face. He actually grinned. "Nope. Sure don't. In fact, I'd have to say it's about time."

Grace was having a hard time closing her mouth, which became impossible as Zee winked and turned to leave without any explanation as to this seemingly abrupt change in his opinion of her.

She followed his descent down the church steps, never taking her gaze off his back as the man who had spent the past month telling everyone in town that she didn't belong here, met up with a familiar face at the bottom of those concrete steps before strolling away arm in arm with none other than Mary Francis.

Grace blinked, her thoughts a whirl as to what that meant, what to think, what to say when—

"Haney?" Where Zee—Zophiel, Grace corrected—and Mary Francis had stood only moments before, Chief Daniels now occupied the space, and there was something foreboding in both his voice and his pained expression.

"Chief." Seeming to detect that same tension, a sense of dread, really, Colin brushed a hand down Grace's arm and linked his fingers with hers before heading down to where the man stood.

Chief Daniels glanced at their joined hands before nodding and offering Grace a "Good morning," then with a tug on his earlobe, he turned to give Colin his full attention.

"I'm sorry to do this now, Haney, but it's about Hank."

"Hank?" Grace piped in. Confused, she glanced from one to the other. "I didn't realize you knew him."

Colin furrowed his brow. "Hank is Camdyn, my brother. Cam didn't play sports, but I did, and Daniels here was the coach—still is—and he's always called everyone by their last names."

The police chief chimed in, interrupting Colin's explanation. "So, of course, Colin here has always been 'Haney' to me. Then when I started having to deal with his brother who was more and more often getting himself into scrapes of one kind or another, two Haneys would have been confusing, so Camdyn became 'Hank.'"

Surely, her Hank couldn't be the same person, she mused.

Tightening her grip on Colin's hand, Grace studied his face, searching for any resemblance. Hank was darker, both his hair and his eyes, his personality, certainly. But now that she was looking, there *was* something similar about the shape of their mouths, the length of their noses... And the way both teased...

Colin asked, "What's going on, Chief?"

Daniels took a deep breath. "There was an accident late last night out on the highway, about twenty miles outside of town. No one was hurt, thank God, but a couple managed to flip their camper into a ravine, and Mac was called to the scene to haul it back out," he added, nodding to his left where Lizbeth and Duncan stood with the twins talking to some of their neighbors. Mackenzie and her Aunt Virginia were among them, and looking them over, Grace realized then that Mac was dressed in her work clothes, looking like she hadn't slept in days. Obviously, Mac hadn't been present in church this morning and had just arrived along with the chief, who wore his usual policemen's uniform.

Continuing, Daniels said, "She was hooking their camper up, getting ready to pull it out when something down in the river below caught Mac's eye. A glare from something shiny, she said."

Colin stiffened, glanced over at his parents, then back to the officer. "Spit it out, Daniels. What did she find?"

The police chief shuffled his feet and tugged on his ear again. "Well, took us a while to confirm it, but it's Hank's old Plymouth. Appears he was heading in this direction and—"

"When?" Colin asked, cutting him off, while Grace could do nothing more than gasp.

"Not recent is my guess. The highway patrol guys are still out there taking pictures and reconstructing, but I'd say months, maybe even close to a year."

Everything in Colin went limp. His fingers loosened, and his hand dropped to his side. Then, after glancing over to where his parents still stood, he hurried toward them.

Grace stood there stunned for a moment longer, then without thinking, she turned and ran.

She ran all the way to the center of the park, sprinting toward the bridge without stopping. By the time she reached the top, her breath heaved, and her sides ached.

She turned in every direction, searching, and just as her first sob escaped, Hank appeared at the base of the bridge.

He grinned up at her with that typical cocky grin of his. Almost afraid of what she would learn, Grace started toward him. Her steps were hesitant and slow, but with each one, a word, a conversation they'd shared over the past weeks, became clearer.

Hank tilted his head, then with a long, drawn-out sigh, he leaned back against the railing in his usual pose, his arms folded over his chest.

"I've been here a while, Gracie, waiting for you. Took you long enough to come to this point."

"Hank—"

He raised a hand and begged her to let him do the talking.

Settling in, he began, "You know, day after day, hour after hour, I've sat here, and I've watched. I've seen children play, couples stroll arm in arm looking sappy. People, unlike you, living their lives. I've been witness to sorrow, but little of that's visible from here, and I've had the occasional pleasure of observing some mischief now and then or listening in on the rare tale of someone's *misdeeds*. But mostly, I've spent this time surrounded by the life you and I both have refused to live."

Grace opened her mouth to speak, but Hank put up a hand again.

"I've seen love bloom," he continued, "watched it endure, and I've seen true happiness in the faces that pass me every day. Those things are all around me here, minute upon minute and hour upon hour, reminding me, taunting me with what I refused to hold on to in my own life.

"Because once upon a time, *I had it, Gracie*," he said, clenching his fist. "I know you haven't, and that's a damn shame, but I did, and then I selfishly tossed it aside."

His grin widened, and Hank resumed his standard negligent pose. "So, in the end, I got what I had coming to me. I guess you could say I was... *condemned*, for lack of a better word, to sitting here, watching and thinking."

"Thinking?" she questioned. "About what?"

Hank frowned. "Choices, I'd say. And I did just that, Gracie, I watched, and I learned a great deal about choices."

She stared at him, not knowing what to say, but Hank didn't appear to want her to say anything, so instead, she listened, and she let him talk.

"I watched them—Alec and Ainsley and my little brother, who without hesitation, stepped up and took my place.

"And so now I see what was offered and what I threw away because *I* gave up, Gracie. I gave up the right to call them my own, even though I can't help but still think of them as mine.

"And so I spent this time thinking. Thinking and wondering what my life would have been like had I made better choices.

"Would I have been the kind of dad I was raised to be if I'd given it half a chance? Would I have eventually followed in Mom and Pop's footsteps or just continued down that same destructive path?"

He grinned that self-deprecating grin that she'd come to know so well. "I torched my bridges, God knows," he said with a laugh. "I made some enemies, a few friends, and not the best kind of friends, either. But most of all, I left a lot of disappointment in my wake, so it certainly came as no surprise when I found myself stuck in this limbo, halfway between Heaven and Hell. Stuck here on Earth with no way to feel or be felt. Neither seen nor heard. With no connection at all.

"Until you, that is.

"And watching you, Gracie... Watching you live the same way, the same half-existence, taught me more in just a few weeks than I'd learned in all the time I've spent here.

"And not that it does me a damn bit of good now, but do you want to know what I'm taking from what you've taught me, Gracie, what lesson I've learned?"

She shook her head.

"That it's never too late until it is."

EPILOGUE

Christmas Eve
One Year and Two Days Later

Grace tip-toed into the bedroom dressed in her favorite satin nightgown with its matching robe flapping open at her sides.

From his crossed-legged spot on the floor, Colin glanced up from his task and smiled. "Get them all tucked in?"

"Finally," she said with a sigh as she dropped down onto a corner of the mattress. "Ainsley had to have just one more story, and that was after the three I'd already read for them. Then it took another ten minutes to convince Alec that no, Santa Claus would not skip the Pulaski household even though Faith swore to her boys—in the presence of other children, I might add—that she had every intention of standing guard outside their house all night so she could tell Santa he had the wrong address if the jolly elf dared to even *think* about leaving them something."

Colin laughed, then lifted a stray part and examined it with a twist of his lips.

"How's that coming?" Grace asked, indicating the dollhouse that looked to be just about finished.

"If I could just figure out what this is and where it goes..."

"Let me see." As Colin held it up for her inspection, Grace put a hand to her swollen belly and leaned close. "It's the doorbell, so I'd imagine it goes somewhere on the front facade."

"Oh." Colin gave the piece a frown before turning the house around and finding just the spot.

Half an hour later, with the last of the gifts tucked under the tree, they sat cuddled together on the living room sofa with only the colorful lights of the tree for illumination, enjoying warm milk and cookies, and one of their all too rare moments of quiet time.

After spending a long moment staring at the framed photograph of his brother—just one of many displayed around the house—Colin set it back in its place on the end table.

"He knows," Grace said, guessing at the thoughts running through Colin's mind. "Hank knows you've forgiven him."

"You think so?"

"I know so."

Colin couldn't help but grin at her ever-growing faith. At how she could instantly make everything better whenever he faltered in his own. He wrapped an arm around her shoulders and asked for a bedtime story.

But Grace wasn't having it. "I think it's *your* turn to tell *me* one."

"Okay," he said with a forced, put-upon sigh, "if you insist."

"I do." Resting her head on his shoulder, Grace snuggled in.

"Let me see..." he began. "Did I ever tell you *why* I begged you to marry me?"

"No," she replied, not bothering to hold back a giggle.

"Well, there was the fact that I was madly in love with you, of course, and my parents and the twins who loved you just as madly."

"'*Loved?*'" she interrupted.

"*Loved* then and love even more today," he assured her with a tender squeeze and kiss on the head. "But then you know that part.

What you don't know is how Allie threatened to never speak to me again if I didn't get on with it, while Charlie took another route. He promised me an employee discount for life if I convinced you to make St. Thad your permanent home."

"Such pressure," she teased.

"Oh, that was only half of it. Virginia May made sure to put her two cents in as well. She said I was a damn fool if I waited one more day, and Mac followed that by threatening to knock me over the head with whatever car part she was holding at the time. I can't tell you what it was, but I can assure you it would have done some damage. Then there was Pat who swore I'd have to do without his famous meatballs for at least a year if I didn't get down on one knee before Valentine's Day." Grace laughed so hard she had to hold on to her bouncing belly, prompting Colin to brush her hands away and give the protruding mound a circular rub.

Once she caught her breath, Grace asked, "And how on Earth could you have lived without Pat's meatballs for an entire year?"

"*Exactly,* Colin said with emphasis. "Which is why *that* one was the clincher."

NEXT UP IN THE
HALO CHRISTMAS SERIES

INSPIRING FAITH

A Note from the Author

As I said in my Dedication, my daughter is a lover of all things Christmas, but then, so am I. Along with hoarding a stack of Christmas-themed books to read. Every year, we take a girls' weekend and go Christmas shopping. We spend the night (sometimes two) in a hotel while we're at it, and stay up as late as we can keep our eyes open, modifying our lists and watching Christmas movies. We even make a habit of calling or texting throughout the season to remind the other not to forget to record that new Hallmark Christmas movie! So, naturally, I just *had* to write a Christmas book. And when the idea for the Town of St. Thaddaeus hit, it of course, came to me as a series.

Although in Redeeming Grace, my main character was raised a Catholic, you may have noticed that I did not base the town nor my angels strictly on the Catholic faith. Of the many angel names used, some come from Christianity as a whole, while others Judaism, Islam, and even Jewish mythology. This is my way of showing you that although the townspeople who founded St. Thaddaeus were a mixture of many faiths, their belief in angels was just one of the many things they had in common.

Another tidbit I want to share is that when creating the Town of St. Thaddaeus, just for some added fun for me in the process, I borrowed from my childhood and family ties. Virginia and Florence, for instance, are both modeled after relatives of mine, while Haney's Hardware and Appliances, Carmine's Barber Shop, and Pat's Hoagies are all based on family-related businesses.

I plan to add more bits of family and childhood memories throughout the series as well, so stay tuned.

Merry Christmas,
Gina

Made in the USA
Middletown, DE
13 November 2021

52169223R00125